HER HONORABLE HERO

A BLACK DAWN NOVEL BOOK 7

CAITLYN O'LEARY

I'm re-dedicating this book to the bravest and kindest person I know, my sister Molly.
You are amazing.

To all who are serving or who have served.
Thank you for your sacrifice and dedication.

1

GRIFF CAUGHT HER AS SHE WAS FLYING OUT OF THE nursery. Miranda was checking the messages on her phone, so the sneak attack was easy.

"What?—" It was impressive how she was able to keep ahold of her phone, even as he whisked her up into his arms and carried her to their bedroom.

"The babysitter is going to be here in thirty-three minutes, we don't have time for your shenanigans."

Being the Type A that she was, his wife was already dressed and ready to go for their night out, so they *definitely* had time. What's more, Griff needed to take care of her. Even though she wouldn't admit it in a million years, she was stressed.

He settled against the plush velvet backboard of their bed, and cradled his gorgeous wife in his arms. He plucked the cell phone out of her hand, and sighed when he saw it was her work e-mail.

"Babe, it's Saturday night."

"We're running over-budget," she protested.

He tossed the phone onto the nightstand. Both of their phones had cases that could withstand hurricanes, so she didn't wince when it bounced.

"So what's this all about?" She crossed her arms over her chest, trying to convey authority. It was a cute move considering he had her cuddled against his chest.

Griff stroked his hand over her soft hair, continuing down her back until he reached the top of her ass. He kept doing this until she sighed with pleasure. Even after three years together, whenever Miranda was nervous her walls slammed up and she tried to handle things on her own. But it was his duty *and* pleasure to remind her he had her six.

"Do we have to go?" she asked in a quiet voice.

"Absolutely not. Say the word, and I'll make a call, and we stay home. Or we go out since we have a babysitter. We just don't go down to Del Mar."

"You'd do that? Even though they expect us?"

"Hell, say I got pulled away on a mission, blame it all on me. They'd buy that." She wouldn't go for his suggestion. She never did, but he'd do it in a heartbeat for this amazing woman.

"No, I can't let them down." She sounded forlorn.

"It's not your job to make everyone happy. They'll have the party and have fun, whether you're there or not."

"They're expecting me," she cuddled closer and bit her lip. "It's just that I hate it."

"Sweets, I know you do. As much as you like to kick ass and take names, when it comes to taking praise, you would prefer to have bamboo shoots shoved under your fingernails."

Miranda stroked the silk of his gray tie. "That's not true." She let her fingers slip between the buttons of his dress shirt. He grabbed her busy hand and brought it to his mouth, and kissed the tips of her dainty fingers.

"See, even when I bring it up, it kills you. You're deflecting."

She stiffened in his arms, just like she always did when he brought up this subject. Even after knowing each other over three years, and being married two-and-a-half, there was a part of herself that Miranda kept locked up tight. Griff tried to respect it, but lately it gnawed at him like a sore tooth.

"We have twenty-nine minutes," she murmured.

He'd started out wanting to seduce her. Hell, when did he not want to make love to Miranda? But now he wanted to talk, and she was trying to use sex to halt the conversation. Part of him was tempted to push for dialogue. Then she started to unbutton his shirt.

Miranda looked up at him through the fringe of her lashes as her tongue swirled against his chest.

Holy mother of God. She knew him so well.

"Miranda," he tried to take control. "Talk to me, Baby. If you feel like you need to go, tell me why it's so hard for you and maybe I can make it easier."

She unbuttoned more buttons and speared her fingers through his chest hair.

"It's not a big deal, I'll be fine." She pulled his tie loose and tossed it.

It was *a big deal, dammit.*

A delicate brush of her tongue across his nipple and he was done. His lids lowered and all thought was focused on the most beautiful woman in the world. She was. He'd thought so the moment he'd seen her on the train, and nothing had ever changed his mind.

Griff easily lifted her up and away from him.

"No," she quietly wailed. "I liked that."

"Then you'll really like this," he promised.

He gave a feral smile when her legs trembled as he stood her up beside the bed. "Easy," he said.

She slammed her hands on his shoulders, her short pink nails digging into his dress shirt. Griff enjoyed the little sting. He enjoyed it so much, he reached up and tangled his fingers in her hair and pulled her head down for a mind-numbing kiss. He didn't stop until she was plastered against his chest and his ears were ringing with her gasps.

Griff pulled one hand off his shoulder and tugged the long sleeve of her blue dress down her supple arm, then he repeated the process on the other side.

Fuck. She was wearing a bustier. *His* bustier. The one he'd picked out for her. How had he not noticed?

He reached around to start taking it off.

"It'll take too long, and it takes forever to get it back on. We need to leave it on," she whispered against his ear.

"Jesus, Miranda. Are you trying to kill me? If I get any more turned on, I'll end up with zipper burn on my dick."

His woman bit his earlobe as she giggled. "We don't

want to damage the equipment. I'm in great need of your dick."

Griff chuckled as he moved his hands and slid her dress over her hips, pulling the thin wisp of lace along with it. Miranda took a dainty step out of her clothes and tried to bend down to pick them up.

"Leave it."

"It'll wrinkle," she protested.

"It won't be on the floor long enough to wrinkle," he promised.

"Eyes on me," she commanded. She meant that she wanted him to look her in the eye. She'd been saying that since the baby. Silly woman was still feeling insecure about her curves.

"My eyes are on you," Griff said as he leaned forward and kissed her stomach. His fingers trailed lightly along her pelvis. She shivered. She'd always been sensitive there, and he wasn't going to stop touching his favorite places, especially when, in his eyes, they were even more beautiful.

He trailed kisses lower, then twisted them around so that she was the one sitting on the bed and he was on his knees in front of her. He looked up her body, relishing the look of her black hair spread out on the white sheets and her breasts heaving inside her black bustier. She was a goddess.

"Griffin?"

"Right here, Babe."

He parted her legs slowly, looking his fill. Damn right, men were visual creatures, and wasn't he blessed with something this gorgeous to look at?

"Griffin, stop playing." Miranda was getting pissy. Just another thing that turned him on. Ms. High Powered Executive got his motor running every damn time. Well, two could play at this game.

He looked at her over her breasts hidden under the bustier, and raised an eyebrow. "Really? That's the way you want to play it?" He stroked one broad finger down the delicate flesh that was driving him insane.

She whimpered. Then cleared her throat. "I said stop playing." There was still a bite to her words.

He grinned. Obviously he needed to try harder. He raked his teeth along the top of her right thigh.

This time she moaned. "Oh yeah."

Gone was the Ms. Project Manager. He licked her in a way he knew would drive her crazy.

"Is this what you wanted?" he asked.

He heard her 'yes' hiss out.

He repeated the caress, determined to drive her higher. Determined to give her pleasure and comfort before the party.

"Griffin" She sobbed. "Please don't tease. Not tonight."

Was her voice clogged with tears? He could count on one hand the number of times Miranda had cried.

He surged up off his knees and was cradling her head in a heartbeat. He saw the telltale tear tracks at her temples. "Talk to me," he demanded.

Miranda shook her head wildly. "I need to be close to you. To know I'm yours. I need to know you'll never leave."

Where the fuck was this coming from?

"I'm here, Baby." He whispered a kiss along her temple, and trailed it down her jaw, then he rested his forehead on hers. "You've got me. Forever or worse, in sickness and health, no matter the fuck what. Remember? They'd have to use the jaws of life to *attempt* to pry me away, and that wouldn't even work. Got it?"

Her mouth wobbled, then firmed.

Miranda's hands fumbled at his belt, and he helped her. She didn't go easy on his engorged flesh, she stroked hard.

Damn.

Griff shoved off his pants and touched his wife once again. She might be eager, and so was he, but he would always make sure she was ready for him. He groaned. She felt like liquid silk.

She raked her teeth over his shoulder and he sank deep.

Miranda opened eyes that were more violet than blue, her lashes tipped with tears. "I'm going to need you forever," she whispered.

Softly, slowly, thoroughly, he blended their bodies together. He watched with satisfaction as Miranda began to take comfort and joy in his arms. He slid his hands downward so that he could caress her breasts, the feel of her heating his blood as it lit a fire in Miranda's eyes. So beautiful.

He layered a kiss on her swollen lips and they clung together, their bodies knew one another and they shifted ever upwards, until Miranda's movements became frantic.

Griff gloried in her need, his hands travelling down to grasp her hips tight against him so that they were locked together. She threw her head back and he licked his tongue along her arched neck, savoring the taste of her sweet skin.

Miranda dug her fingernails into his ass and he gritted his teeth. He thrust in a way that he knew would bring her the most pleasure. She opened her mouth, then clamped it shut before any sound could be heard.

If she had that much restraint, he wasn't doing it right. Griff moved his hand and touched the bud of her clit.

"No," she wailed softly. "It's too much. I can't."

"Yes you can," he whispered. Griff was determined to last. He circled her swollen flesh and watched her wanton expression. He kept her on edge, then finally he surged upwards and pinched softly. This time she couldn't stop her cry of release.

His body rushed over the edge into oblivion. His wife always took him to the stars.

Long moments later, he felt the sting of his hair being pulled. Ms. Executive was back and she was lifting his head off her bustier so she could look him in the eye.

"You're one determined man, Mr. Porter."

"And that's a problem, why?"

She looked over his shoulder at the nightstand. "All I've got to say is, thank God for closed doors and baby monitors."

"You should be thanking God that the United States Navy trains their men to be prepared."

2

GRIFF AND MIRANDA ARRIVED A HALF HOUR LATE TO THE amazing house in La Jolla. It was the second time they had been to Leslie Bell's house. Her best friend had been Carol Shepard who had died during the wreck on the Amtrak train three years ago. This was a celebration of life not just for Carol, but for the others whose lives had been lost. Leslie took it upon herself to host the event to celebrate the heroes. Miranda looked at the house with trepidation, because unfortunately she knew that in the eyes of most people, she was considered the ultimate hero, and she *hated* that.

She wasn't a damn hero. She had been acting on instinct that day. She'd been scared out of her mind. She'd told everybody that until she was blue in the face, but they wouldn't listen. Hell, she was married to a true hero, someone who had signed up to serve his country and put his life on the line time after time. Griff and his team were the heroes.

She sighed.

"I heard that. It's not too late. We haven't gotten to the front of the drive, I think only the valet has seen us at this point."

"Oh yeah, I forgot. Only Leslie has a valet at her house," Miranda laughed.

Griff slowed the car to a stop at the top of the circular drive, long before they got to the door. "I'm serious, Miranda, we can go home now."

"Nope. I promised Susan we'd be there. She said Hope has a surprise for me. I won't let her down."

"I love that girl. Not as much as Livvie, but close. Damn close," Griff smiled warmly.

"Well, get driving."

As the car started up again, her stomach lurched and she gritted her teeth.

Get over yourself. You're a grown-ass woman. Quit with the fucking phobias.

Soon they were walking up the granite staircase to the massive doors flung open in welcome. Tea lights guided them through the house toward the array of French doors that opened to a huge deck, swimming pool and yard. So much land for one person's home in Southern California always made Miranda's mind boggle.

"Randa!"

"Her name's Mira," Jeremy corrected his little sister. Both of the Thompson children came running and Griff put his arm around her so that she was braced for the mini hurricane when they hit her.

"I have a s'prise for you, Randa," Hope lisped. At five years old, she'd lost her two front teeth.

"*Your* present has to wait," Jeremy said, with the authority that only an older brother of seven could provide.

Miranda smiled up at Griff who was struggling not to laugh.

Mike Thompson walked up with a German beer and handed it to Griff. "Sorry man, there's not a Pacifico to be found. Leslie figures we all have high-brow taste."

Susan walked up and put her arm around her newly-minted husband. "Both of you do have high-brow taste, you married us."

Susan winked at Miranda when the two men clinked their bottles. Miranda loved her friend. They sure as hell had been through the fires of hell together. When Miranda had had an opening for a staff assistant at her TAID, she immediately thought of Susan. She knew that the woman would be a great fit because she was familiar with how the military worked, since her deceased husband had been part of an Army unit in Afghanistan.

Miranda had been working for Technological Applied Integrated Data since she'd graduated with her masters. She loved it at TAID, because as a technology integrator that consulted for diverse clients throughout the world, she was never bored. Her expertise was project management and she had a flair for liaising with the military complex and civilian companies. Most of her work varied from classified to top secret.

"Come on, Missy," Susan said, grabbing Miranda's arm. "It's time for you to make the rounds."

Griff's arm tightened around her waist.

"Want me to go with you?" he whispered against her ear.

She shook her head, and started to let Susan lead her away. The sun was setting over the Pacific Ocean and a lot of the guests were leaning against the deck rail, watching the sizzling splash of colors light the sea and sky.

"Wait Mom, where are the flowers?" Jeremy called out.

"Oh I'm sorry, Honey. They're over by Leslie. Come with us."

"What flowers?" Miranda asked Susan.

Jeremy heard her question. "Hope has to wait til after dinner for her present. You get mine now." He ran past them and leaped down the steps into the yard toward a ring of redwood chairs surrounding a firepit.

"Mrs. Bell! Where are the flowers for Mira?"

Miranda could hear Leslie's laugh float toward them. By the time they got to where Jeremy was, he was practically jumping up and down with excitement. He was standing in front of one of the chairs and as Miranda got closer, he jumped to the side and then she froze.

"Ta-da!" Jeremy shouted.

She stared at the bouquet of flowers.

"Do you like them Mira? I picked them out. You're pretty like the sun. So I got you yellow flowers." Miranda had to look closer to realize they were large Gerber Daisies and not sunflowers. But even that didn't dispel the feeling of dread.

"Miranda, are you okay?" Susan looked from her to

the flowers and back again. Then she laughed. "I steered him away from the sunflowers because I know those are special to you." She laughed and nudged her with her elbow.

"Yeah. Special." Miranda said sickly. Thank God it was dusk so Susan couldn't get a good look at her expression.

"Mira? Aren't you happy?"

Oh Bloody Hell.

Miranda crouched down. "Jeremy, this is a wonderful present! I love my flowers!"

His grin was huge.

"You're going to like my present, too," Hope said from behind her. "It's a s'prise," she said again.

"You two are so special, I'm going to love both of your presents as much as the whole wide world," Miranda threw out her arms out wide.

Hope giggled and Jeremy's grin just got bigger.

"Hey, I think I see some of the kids getting in the bouncy house," Susan said. Both of her kids' heads spun to take a look across the lawn.

"Can we go?" Jeremy begged.

"Yep. Just be sure to come out when your Dad tells you to. Got it?"

"We promise," Hope said as she grabbed her brother's hand and started to drag him across the grass.

"God I love your kids," Leslie said as she got up and moved the flowers off the chair. "Your son Jeremy is going to be a heartbreaker."

"He is growing up so fast. He wants to be Mike when he grows up."

"That's a pretty good aspiration if you ask me," Betty said.

"You two are a sight for sore eyes." Miranda said as she sank down in the now empty chair.

"I think she's talking about the sangria," Leslie said as she lifted the pitcher. She picked up an empty glass, poured a hefty amount and handed it to Miranda.

Miranda took a small sip. She needed it after the flower incident. She needed to keep herself together. She really couldn't take much more.

She took a deep breath, and then smiled. Okay, enough wallowing, she was here with dear friends, she was going to enjoy herself.

"I was waiting for you to get here," Betty beamed. "I wanted to show you something."

Miranda looked at the middle-aged woman. She'd retired from Amtrak soon after the wreck. She'd been smart enough to get some counselling for her PTSD after the accident. No moss grew under that stone.

"Does that something have anything to do with those gorgeous diamonds you've been trying to hide?" Leslie asked as she crossed her legs.

"Dammit, nothing gets by you," Betty grumbled. Then she gave a delighted laugh and thrust her hand out. "Look at this. Jared gave it to me. When we got married thirty-five years ago, he could only afford a wedding band. I was stunned when he bought me this eternity ring." She looked at it lovingly. Miranda couldn't be happier for the woman, then she started to laugh again. "Of course he bought it from a diamond store called Jared."

"If there was a diamond store called Mike's, you can be damn sure my husband would have bought my ring there. Instead I just get subs from Mike's Sandwich Shop. He loves bringing home the bag with the Mike's logo."

Leslie gave Miranda a sisterly smile. Apparently she knew that neither Griff nor her husband were bringing home bags with their names on them. But...

"I will say, considering the bags Griff brings home, you'd think my name was Victoria," Miranda whispered to Leslie.

"I heard that," Susan called out. She motioned toward her breasts, "you need to have two kids, then you'll start getting bags from Fredericks of Hollywood."

Miranda let out a loud laugh, and for the first time that night, she thought she might get through the event without throwing up.

"I think we're missing out on all the fun," Griff said as he came up behind their hostess. Leslie twisted in her chair to see who was talking. "Susan was doing some interesting pantomime. Mike and I wanted to see what was going on.

Susan turned bright red.

Miranda looked over at Mike. It was fifty-fifty whether he would tease his wife or cover for her.

"Susan, care to share with the class?" Leslie asked.

"Yeah, Susan, we saw some funny hand signals going on when we were walking up. This should be fun," Mike teased his wife.

"I was explaining how puffed up your chest got when I told you I would marry you."

Miranda loved how quick-witted her friend was. Her ability to think on her feet made her an outstanding assistant.

Mike reached out and grabbed Susan's hand and brought it to his lips. "You're right about that. I still don't think that's what you were talking about," his voice trailed off.

Susan gave him a smile that was the picture of innocence. "Can't prove it."

Watching the love between Mike and Susan made Miranda think of another man who was missing. "Did you hear from Josiah?" Miranda asked Leslie.

"Captain Hale said he couldn't make it," Leslie sighed. "But, Billy Anderson is here," she smiled brightly. "I can't believe how much he has grown up."

"Where is he?" Mike asked.

"He's in the game room. Drake's showing him how to shoot pool," she laughed.

"That should be interesting, I think I'll go check it out." Mike nodded and smiled before he headed toward the house.

"Tell the boys that the buffet will be ready in a half hour, will you?" she asked.

Mike gave her a wave over his head. "I'm on it."

Betty called Griff over to show off her ring, and Leslie took the opportunity to lean. "You didn't answer your phone tonight," she admonished Miranda.

"What?"

"I tried to call and warn you. I wanted to keep things low-key. I noticed things got kind of dicey for you last year, so I wanted to tone it down this year. No speeches, just a little get-together, but we have a problem." Leslie's eyes darted over to Susan, then she lowered her voice even more.

"Susan had Mason's wife make a cake and Hope wrote a story that she wants to read to people."

"Hope?" Miranda said with dismay. "But she's only five."

"I'm pretty sure Jeremy helped. They worked on it at school."

Miranda's heart sank. What had that special little girl come up with? She set her glass down and pushed up from her chair.

"Where are you going?" Griff asked.

"I think I'm going to go in and check on the guys. Maybe Billy can show me his new moves."

Her husband nodded.

MIRANDA COULDN'T EAT MUCH at dinner, her stomach was too fluttery. But the little she had eaten sat like a lump. Please God, say she'd make it through this last little bit.

There were too many people to contain inside the house, but Leslie had cleverly arranged things so that the living room and deck were one great big space with the French doors flung open. It really was an extraordinary home. She'd even arranged for a mini stage that Hope and Jeremy could make themselves comfortable on. It was elevated enough so that even if the children sat down on the two chairs provided, everyone could see them easily.

Where was Griffin?

"Randa! Daddy, come here." Hope shouted. Her little voice reverberated around the room. Shit, Leslie even had the little girl mic'd. Miranda stood frozen. She felt beads of sweat pop on her forehead as she plastered a fake smile on her face. The only good thing was that she had used the world's best deodorant and her dress was dark, otherwise everybody would know she was a nervous, sweaty mess.

"I've got you," Griff whispered softly against her temple as his arm slid around her waist. "It's going to be okay."

With him beside her, it would be somewhat better, but it would take a hell of a lot for it to hit the 'okay' level.

"Let's do this." She looked up at him. She saw his frown when he saw her pseudo-smile.

"Randa. Hurry."

She took a step forward, but Griff stilled her progress. "One last thing." He cupped her cheek, and feathered his thumb over her bottom lip. Then her man with the chocolate eyes bent down and touched his lips against hers. His kiss was reverent, a solemn moment between the two of them. Miranda trembled, his tender caress gave her courage.

"I've got this," she said. She started to believe it.

"Jeremy, them's kissin'," Hope whispered. But her whisper was heard all the way out to the people at the back of the deck, and Miranda closed her eyes and groaned at the laughter.

"Your subjects await, M'Lady," Griff grinned down at her. He gently nudged her forward and people parted as they made their way to the front of the great room.

"You two stand next to Mom and Dad," Hope pointed. It was cute seeing the miniature Susan with her long brown curls and pink velvet dress, directing traffic. Jeremy just watched on, his look both indulgent and long-suffering. He was a good big brother. He always had been.

Miranda leaned into Griff's powerful frame and smiled up at the children. Hope was clutching one of those huge pieces of lined paper from grade school in one hand, and waving at her with her other.

Miranda waved back.

"I wrote a story. Jeremy helped me." Hope's lisp was adorable, but Miranda wondered how much of the story she was really going to be able to read, since she was only five.

"Jeremy. Hold the story, so I can read." The little girl thrust the stapled papers at her brother's chest and he rolled his eyes in exasperation. He held up the paper at Hope's eye level, and the smart boy managed to position it so that his sister's smile was facing the audience.

Hope cleared her throat, and peered around the room.

"I named this story, Heroes." She grinned and pointed at Miranda. "She's a hero." Then her arm swung and she pointed to Mike Thompson. "So's my new Daddy. He's a hero, too. There's more. But them two's the biggest. I'm goin' to 'splain."

Miranda saw the pride shining off the little girl, and it was so contrary to what she was feeling. She wanted a big hole to appear under her and swallow her up. She peeked over at Mike to see if he was as embarrassed as she was, but he was beaming up at his two stepchildren. His delight in them was palpable.

"A long, long time ago, Mommy took me and Jeremy on a train ride. It was a long, long ride."

"That part's not in the story," Jeremy whispered.

"But it was a long ride." Hope said as she pulled down on her pink dress. Then she bent down and adjusted the heel of her black patent Mary Jane shoe, which caused her dress to ride up again. She carefully pulled down her dress, then pushed the curls away from her face with both hands.

"Where was I?" she asked her brother.

"You said it was a long ride," he pointed to a point on the paper. "You need to start here. It says—"

"I know. I mem-rized." She turned and faced everyone again and waved. "Jeremy helped. He wrote down the words, and I practiced them. Okay." She thrust out her little hands and bent her knees. "It gets scary now." She wasn't looking at her brother or the paper anymore.

Miranda was getting caught up in the little girl's performance.

"The train crashed. It made a big noise and everything turned black. Nobody could see." She bent down even lower, her eyes wide. She flattened her hands and aimed them at the floor. "Jeremy got losted from Mommy, and Mommy got hurt. Jeremy was scared because he couldn't find her."

The paper in Jeremy's hand trembled. Miranda looked at the boy and saw that his face was pale. She remembered that terrifying moment when she woke up to darkness, when it was just her and Jeremy trapped under the train seat.

"But Mommy found my brother, but her leg got broke." Hope pointed down to her mother's leg. "I member her in a cast. I made a flower on it."

She stopped. You could have heard a pin drop in the room. Not a single ice cube clinking could be heard.

"Jeremy?" Hope turned to her brother.

He took a moment to respond. "Huh?"

"What's the next words?"

Jeremy carefully turned the page of the stapled papers. He pressed the corner tight.

"It says you disappeared, Hope."

Hope whirled around and faced the group of fascinated listeners. "I got losted. Nobody could find me. Mommy was hurted and couldn't get off the train and we needed the Marines like my Daddy."

"What about the Navy?" someone called out from the back.

"No," she shook her head emphatically, making her curls swing around her face. "Just Marines like my Daddy," Hope said firmly.

Loud laughter sounded throughout the room.

Hope looked around in surprise. She looked down

at her parents for reassurance, and when she saw Mike give her a thumbs-up, she started to laugh, too. When the chuckling finally subsided, the same voice that had called out about the Navy shouted out for Hope to continue. Miranda was pretty sure it was Wyatt Leeds, a member of Griff's SEAL team.

"My mom 'splained that the train was tipped over. It took lots of strong mens to pull it up. But I was losted. I was probably looking for my family, so I crawled outside. Everyone was looking for me."

She turned to Jeremy. "Was I crying or was I brave like you?"

Jeremy was clearly dazed by the question. Miranda looked over at Susan, and she saw her friend had a similar look as her son. Hope's childlike account of the terror was too much for both of them. Miranda remembered the exact moment she'd spotted Hope's tiny form outside the train. Joy and panic had poured through her at that moment, a similar torrent of emotion that was flooding through her right now.

Mike maneuvered Susan next to Miranda. "Stay close," he whispered to them both. Then he bounded up onto the stage and pulled his two children close to his chest, his head bending down low.

"Dad, I don't know if I was brave," Jeremy's forlorn whispered words echoed across the room through his mic.

"You are the strongest little man I know." Mike's voice didn't need a microphone.

Jeremy's big eyes stared up at the man he clearly

adored. A look of profound understanding passed between them, and the boy smiled.

Hope wiggled in her father's hold. "I needs to tell the rest of the story."

Mike grinned. He raised one of his knees so that his little girl could hop on, and she settled herself, then she turned to her brother and thrust out her hand. "Jeremy, give me the paper."

Hope twisted around and looked at her audience. "The train was broke. My daddy and bunches of you tied rope around it to try to pull it so it wouldn't fall over and splash into the water."

Jeremy leaned across Mike's lap. "Tell about Billy."

Hope grinned. "Billy was a hero too, even though he was just a kid. He helped save people when he was a surfer. He called for help."

Miranda remembered her feeling of relief when she'd seen Billy's bright gold hair on the train.

"But the bestest heroes were my dad and Randa. Dad got my mom off the train and married her."

Laughter roared throughout the crowd, carrying Miranda along with them.

"Why are they laughing?" Hope asked Mike.

"You made it sound like I married your mom that day. I would have too." Mike kissed the top of Hope's head.

Hope frowned, and wagged her finger at her audience. "They had a wedding later. I was a flower girl." She turned over the paper that she plainly wasn't reading from and cleared her throat.

"Daddy saved Mommy. Then somebody had to save

me, cause I was outside the train. I was going to fall a long, long way down into the water." With every word, Hope's voice got softer and softer. "Mommy said that Randa saved me."

Miranda started as Susan grabbed her arm. Miranda leaned into Griff and pulled Susan close, knowing her friend needed comfort as much as she did to get through Hope's story.

"Then what?" Hope asked her brother.

"They got rope," he whispered.

Miranda could feel the bite of the nylon leash digging into her ankle.

Hope's face broke into a grin. "Oh yeah! Randa used a rope to come get me." She threw out her hands, hitting Mike in the face with one. "It was great! There was a helicopter and everything."

Then her little face fell. "But then everyone had to go to the hospital."

"Not me," Jeremy said. "I just visited."

"Randa had to stay the longest. But Uncle Griff stayed a long time with Randa. He married her too, but I wasn't a flower girl cause I was a baby."

Hope held up the now-crumpled paper. "And everyone lived happily ever after."

A thunder of applause shook the room.

Susan let go of her arm, and clasped Miranda's shoulders so that she was looking up into Miranda's face. "I will never, ever forget what you did for my baby. Never." Tears were streaming down her friend's face.

Miranda's stomach hollowed out and she panicked.

"You would have done the same thing for Livvie," she protested.

"Listen to me, Miranda. For once, fucking listen to me." Susan's fingers dug grooves into her shoulders. "You. Are. A. Hero. You're my hero. My children's hero. I love you."

Before Miranda could respond, Mike tugged Susan into his arms.

Thank Fuck.

Griff turned Miranda into his arms, his hand running up and down her back.

"We have cake!" Leslie's voice called out as the lights went out.

3

Hope's story had stirred Griff's memories of meeting Miranda. As he pulled her close in bed and drifted off to sleep, his memories became his dreams that night. He even felt the gentle rocking of the train three years ago.

Griff Porter ran across the station, barely making it on board. He grinned as soon as he stepped onto the train. It wouldn't have been the end of the world if he had arrived a couple of hours late to the Navy base at Coronado, but he sure as hell didn't want to miss an opportunity to see Miranda Slade. This was their time together, and he'd made up his mind that this morning he'd be asking her out. She might not realize it, but she had been targeted by a SEAL, and that meant she belonged to him.

He sauntered down the car and quickly spotted her raven hair. He'd been pretty sure she'd be on this car since they'd been sitting together on this one for the last nine Mondays. As he came upon her, he saw that there was a newspaper lying on the seat beside her. When she saw him walking toward her, she picked it up and motioned toward the empty seat.

Score!

She was on the phone. That was normal, too. The woman did a lot of work when she was on the train. That was fine, he could wait.

Griff made himself as comfortable as he could in the seat. Even here in the business class section the seats didn't easily accommodate his shoulders. He seemed to end up overflowing into her space a little bit. Miranda didn't seem to mind as she flashed him a bright smile, then settled back into her phone call. Griff shamelessly listened in.

Miranda could have easily commanded forces in the Navy. Right now someone was getting their ass handed to them in D.C.

"Doug, this is the third time you have missed something for Energys. We don't have time to set up an entire new process to do a quality control check behind you."

He watched in fascination as she took quick notes on a sheaf of papers.

"I'm confused. I tracked the time you opened the e-mail. It was actually on Monday, not on Wednesday like you just said. So you actually had five days to go over the contracts. Are you telling me that wasn't enough time?"

She was well and truly pissed. Apparently good ole Doug didn't think she would tag her e-mail. Doug didn't sound like the sharpest tool in the shed.

"Is that really the tack you want to take, Doug?" She asked in a soft voice. "Your final answer is that you didn't get enough time to review the documents, is that it?"

The bastard was probably too stupid to realize he should be pissing his pants.

Griff pretended to scratch his face so he could cover his grin, but Miranda's eyes shifted and caught him. Damn, she didn't miss a trick.

"Thank you for your time Doug," she said politely. Too damn politely in Griff's opinion. Again, the bastard should be scared, with a capital 'S'.

She hung up the phone, shaking her head in disgust as she rapidly dialed another number. It went to voicemail.

"Bob, this is Miranda. Doug's off the Energys project. As of now. I'm not telling you how to handle one of your employees, but I'm going to send you all the information you'll need to write him up if you're so inclined. You'll have it by the end of the day. In the meantime, I'm going to need someone else to support Energys. Someone who can actually perform the job."

Griff watched with pleasure and amazement as she powered off her phone.

He raised an eyebrow. "You're disconnecting?"

"Doug's going to bitch to Bob. Bob's then going to call me and beg me to take Doug back. If I take the call, I might actually say that Bob needs to grow a pair." Her blue eyes glittered, and Griff couldn't take his eyes off her.

"I can't believe the little weasel lied to me. And then

he was stupid about it, thinking I wouldn't check up on him. I'm more insulted that he thought I was too stupid to catch him, than I am that he lied." Her pen tapped rapidly against the paper. "Anyway, I won't handle it well when Bob doesn't do his job, so it's best that I don't talk to the man until tomorrow."

"But why turn off the phone? Can't you just let his call go to voicemail when you see his number come up?"

Miranda patted out an imaginary wrinkle in her pencil skirt and looked back up at him. "I'm kind of OCD," she sighed. "If the phone rings, I answer it. I'm just wired that way."

"How many hours a week do you work?"

"Does working during the commute count? How about during dinner and through my lunch?"

"Yep, all of those hours count. So how many?" He watched as she once again brushed at her skirt, this time picking at some lint that wasn't there.

It was time to make a move.

He picked up her delicate hand in his and held it. "Tell me," he coaxed with the smile that he'd seen his dad use effectively on his mom for twenty-eight years.

"It's because of the new client. So about fourteen or sixteen hours a day. But that's when I'm here in San Diego."

"And when you're home in Anaheim on the weekends?" he prodded.

"I cut it back," her eyes shifted down to their clasped hands. A sure sign she was lying.

"Miranda, one-hundred-hour workweeks is too

much. You have to know that. Especially if you've been doing it for over two months."

As soon as the words were out of his mouth, Griff knew he was in trouble. He'd been accused of being too controlling in the past. Women didn't like it. Then there was the fact that Miranda was as Type A as they came. He was doomed.

"Yeah, I know. You're right."

"That's it? You're going to agree with me?"

She gave him a puzzled look, then laughed. "You thought I was going to have a problem with you hitting me with some home truths?"

Damn, he liked her. *Liked* her, liked her. And he'd already been pretty hooked if he'd been pursuing her for nine weeks on a train, but that sentence cinched things.

"I gotta admit Ms. Slade, I thought you might fight me on it," he grinned slowly.

She leaned in with a grin of her own. "Want to know a secret?"

"Sure."

"I like people who'll call me on my shit. I know you're right. I've been doing this pace for almost five months and I'm close to burnout. That's another reason for turning off the phone. But the product is going to hit the market at the end of next month, and I know I'm capable of keeping it together until then, as long as I power down when I know I'm ready to unleash the four horsemen of the apocalypse on someone's ass."

Griff laughed. "So after next month?"

"Then I'm taking my six weeks accrued time-off in

one big lump. I'm going to find a beach, a lake, or just someplace near water, and veg out." She leaned her head back against the seat and peeked over at him beneath her lashes. "So, see? I have a plan. What do you think of that?"

It sucked. Unless it was a beach here in San Diego. Near him.

"Sounds well-thought-out, exactly what I would expect from you. Are there any special people you want to spend those six weeks with?"

Smooth, Porter, really smooth.

"It'll just be me and Captain Morgan for one week. Smooth Rum on a tropical beach."

Griff brushed his thumb along the side of her hand, where their hands were still clasped. He heard her involuntary intake of breath.

Good. Maybe he was getting to her, because God knew she was living under his skin.

Wait? What was she saying?

"...friends."

"Huh?" he asked.

"I said I'd have to scrounge up one of my girlfriends, but all of them fall under the workaholic category, too." Miranda wrinkled her nose. "Seriously, this shit needs to start slowing down." She shoved at her leather computer case with her attractive maroon heel. Griff loved her choice of footwear. Not too high, but sexy nonetheless.

"What about you, Mr. Navy SEAL, how much time do you take off?"

"What about your friend Wendy? I know she's a big

time director, but won't she take time off to go with you to the beach? If not her, what about Penny?"

Miranda stared at him in amazement.

"What, like you're the only one who pays attention?" he chuckled. "Oh I forgot, Penny moved back to Ohio. Still, can't she meet you?"

"Her new job is keeping her hopping," Miranda sighed. "Plus, she just got a puppy. There's no way she'd leave him so soon."

"And Wendy?" Griff probed.

"She's on location. Nope, I'm probably hitting the beach alone. Anyway, I just asked you a question that you're trying to dodge. How much time do you take off?"

"I don't work nearly as much as you do. When we're not deployed, it's a regular forty-hour workweek, but you know that. I'm up in Anaheim every weekend to help Mom out with Dad."

The train lurched and her case slid, she bent and moved it back. Griff wanted to grab her hand back in his, but figured that'd look too needy.

Miranda tilted her head sideways. "How *is* your dad doing?"

Griff thought about how he'd left things that morning. His dad had been downstairs in the hospital bed. The home healthcare worker would be arriving later in the day. "He's doing better. He and I got in a couple of games of Scrabble. There's no way he would have been up for that last week."

"And your mom?"

"She's amazing, as always." Griff thought about his

petite mother who was the glue that kept his large family together.

"When does your aunt arrive from Hawaii?"

"I sure must talk a lot to you." Griff shifted in his seat so he could look directly at Miranda. He was feeling kind of sheepish.

"Actually, you don't at all. I swear I have to play twenty questions every time I want to get the slightest bit of information from you. Like now."

"I'd prefer to talk about your vacation. You're more interesting than I am."

"Don't make me kick you." Instead of following through on her threat, she pushed at him with her shoulder.

Score! More body contact. He'd take that.

"Your aunt?" she prompted.

"Are you sure you were never in the military?"

"Nope, but I do occasionally run projects in conjunction with the Department of Defense, so you learn a few things. Now spill it."

The train gave another lurch, nothing that really would have caused him to lose his equilibrium, but Griff shifted a little anyway so that their sides were brushing up against one another. Miranda relaxed against him.

One more lurch and he'd have Triple Word Score.

"My auntie is going to arrive on Friday. She's Mom's sister. Auntie Lulu would have come sooner, but her youngest just graduated high school. She wanted to be there for the ceremony. Now she intends to stay out here for a month and help Mom out."

"Oh." Miranda shifted back more into her own seat, breaking contact. "I guess I won't be seeing you anymore, then." She sounded disappointed.

Griff felt a ridiculously huge smile bleed over his face. "When is your assignment going to end? The end of next month?" he asked.

"Most likely. Yeah, six weeks." She bit her lip. She had great lips.

"Then Miranda, I'm going to be taking the train for six more weeks."

"You are?"

"Yep. Now that I know how much longer your assignment is, that's how much longer I intend to keep seeing my parents. Or, you could put me out of my misery and agree to go out to dinner with me."

She gave a slow smile. His pulse sped up. Then she frowned and answered slowly. "Griff, I'd really like that. I would, but I don't usually leave the office until eight, or sometimes even nine at night."

"How safe is the parking lot? How late is it when you get to the station in Anaheim?"

Her eyes sparkled. "You just can't help yourself, can you?"

This time he answered slowly. "My mom and my sisters give me a hard time about this, too. But I'm the oldest, it's hard-wired into my DNA."

"I'm a big girl. I know how to take care of myself. Hell, I'm thirty-one. How old are you?"

"Twenty-eight," Griff answered readily.

"Respect your elders. We know what we're doing. I

know to park under the parking lot lights and have people walk me to my car."

He didn't like the 'elders' shot at all. "Does that always work out for you, Miranda?"

He saw she was opening her mouth for another retort and he wanted to kick his own ass. Really? This is how he was going about asking for a date?

Griff threw his hands up in the air. "Do you have a handkerchief?" he asked.

"What?"

Thank God he stopped her before she tore a strip off him. "A handkerchief. I want to wave it in surrender. Seriously, I swear to God I'm usually smoother than this, but thinking of you unprotected woke up my lizard brain."

He continued to keep his arms in the air as she started to laugh.

"Oh for God's sake, lower your hands," she chuckled. "I forgive you and your lizard."

"Do you forgive us enough to go out to dinner? A late dinner?" he qualified.

"You wouldn't mind waiting?" He liked that she sounded as hopeful as he felt.

"Hell, Miranda, I've been taking this train for two months even though my truck has been out of the shop for the last seven weeks. I'd say I wouldn't mind waiting," he laughed.

"You've been really worried about your dad, haven't you? That's what's been really holding you back, hasn't it?"

Nothing got past this woman. Smart turned him on. A lot.

She was right, it had been because of his dad. For some reason he hadn't felt right about pursuing a social life with his dad so sick from the chemotherapy. But now it was a whole new ballgame, his dad was on the mend.

"Yeah, I've been worried about him, but this last week he's turned a corner."

"I'm so happy for you and your family."

"What kind of food do you like?"

"It really doesn't matter." Her blue eyes gleamed. "Food's food. It's the company that matters."

It just got better and better.

"Hi, you two." Griff looked up to see Betty, the ticket taker.

"How are you doing this morning, Beautiful?" Griff asked.

The middle-aged woman gave him a broad smile. She reminded him of one of his mom's friends. She was a sweetheart.

"I see you're still a big 'ole flirt, Mr. Porter."

"I know better than to flirt with a happily-married woman, Betty. How are the grandkids?" Betty looked around the car and saw that it was pretty empty, so she took a moment to answer.

"Colin is starring in the school play and Angela caught a fly ball in her first game."

"That's fantastic," he and Miranda said simultaneously. They looked at one another, and chuckled, but it was Betty who laughed the loudest.

"You two are the best entertainment I have every Monday," she said. Then she left to scan the next person's ticket.

"So, where were we?" Griff asked.

"I was about to question you," Miranda answered. She started to shrug out of her blazer. Griff helped her, admiring the pink silk blouse that she was wearing. There was something about a woman in a business suit that got to him. Then there was the fact that she was wearing pearls. God, half the time he was ready to swallow his tongue. He forced his brain back into gear.

"Fire away."

"What made you decide to become a SEAL? After I met you, I looked it up. That BUD/S training is intense. What makes a person decide to put themselves through something like that?"

Griff hesitated. He didn't normally open up about that. But then again, no woman had ever thought to ask him such a direct question.

"My great-grandfather and two of his brothers were on the beach at Normandy. Papa John died when I was seventeen. I grew up hearing about World War Two. When I was sixteen, he and his brother Alfred were reminiscing and they talked to me about that day. It was horrific. But they were proud. Their brother, Harold, died on Omaha Beach."

Miranda reached out and put her hand on his. He turned his hand so their palms met and their fingers tangled. She was small and delicate compared to him. Light to his dark.

"All three of them enlisted right after Pearl Harbor."

Griff hesitated. "They were something else. I wanted to be just like them."

"I imagine you did." Miranda smiled up at him. The loudspeaker called for the next stop as the train slowed down.

GRIFF JERKED IN HIS SLEEP, waking both himself and Miranda.

"Are you okay?" she asked.

Griff gave her a sleepy smile that made her sigh with pleasure. His warmth enveloped her and she felt protected. "Hope's story made me dream about that morning on the train."

"Did it?" Miranda smiled and stroked Griff's face.

"Yeah. Right up to the stop at San Juan Capistrano Station."

The San Juan Capistrano Mission.

Oh God. Mom.

Miranda did her best to hide her emotions. "Yeah, I remember that part," she kept her voice light-hearted. "Nothing's changed, I still like flirting with you."

"Me too." Griff yawned and drifted back off to sleep. His low breathing soothed her as she nestled closer to his chest. His arm tightened a little around her waist. Even in sleep, he seemed to know when she needed comforting. Miranda waited long moments, listening for the sound of his breath to deepen before she shifted the comforter.

"Babe?" he whispered softly.

A thousand out of a thousand times, and she'd never gotten past him.

"Just need a glass of water." She pressed her palm against his heart. She knew he smiled. He always did when she touched him that way.

"Come back soon," he slurred. Griff dug his fist under his pillow and settled back to sleep. She stood still beside the bed, ensuring his breathing evened out before she grabbed the baby monitor off the dresser and left the bedroom. Even with the monitor in her hand, she couldn't help veering off and checking in on Livvie. Her baby looked just like Griff. People said that their daughter was an amalgamation of the two of them, but she was all Porter. She didn't see any Slade in the little girl. Her big brown eyes, silky black hair and beautiful honey skin, they were all her daddy's. One day they'd take her to Hawaii and she and Griff would look like natives.

Now that she was assured that both of the people she loved were safely asleep, she padded to her little corner of the living room. It was a corner that had a shelf of books, pictures, and a tall window that showed a view of one of the many valleys in the inland area surrounding San Diego. Miranda's chair looked over both the shelf and the window so she could see pictures of Griff, Livvie, his family, and finally, her mom, all juxtaposed by the vastness of nature.

She settled in her oversized chair and put the baby monitor on the shelf, then snuggled against one of the soft plush arms. She plucked up the small picture of Olivia Rose Slade off the bookcase. Her mother hadn't been a big smiler, but by God, Miranda had coaxed one out of her that day, and she'd caught it on film. She loved this picture. It was taken on one of those days they'd visited an old Spanish mission in Southern California.

"I miss you, Mom," she said as she brushed her thumb over her Mom's gentle features.

She loved that her eyes were sparkling, when many times they'd been shadowed. Miranda had known it was because of the utter bastard who had haunted their lives. Her mother always glossed over who and where her father was, trying to get Miranda to believe that he had died before she was born or some such nonsense, but Miranda saw through that like a clear mountain stream. Miranda figured that even if she hadn't had that one memory from when she was around the age of four, she still would have known that her father had done Olivia Slade wrong. But because she'd eavesdropped, she would never forget just how cold, how mean and how evil her father had really been.

Miranda bit her lip and locked the memory back in the depths of her mind, where it belonged. He was nothing to her. Less than nothing.

She moved her focus back to her Mom's smile, that's what was important. This woman who had sacrificed so much for her to have a good life.

"Griff would have knocked your socks off, Mom." She brushed back a tear. "No matter what, I can count on him. And so will Livvie, she'll never doubt for a second that she's loved and protected, Mom. Not one damned second."

Yep, she'd chosen well.

She sat back into her chair and pulled the afghan around her, remembering back to all those days when her man, Griffin Porter, had pursued her. That man had gotten her into his sights, and lasered in. How many times had he told her that story? How he had planned to ask her out that day when everything had started out so perfectly.

Miranda stared long minutes into the moonlit night, thinking about her mom, thinking about the train. Finally sleep found her.

THREE YEARS Earlier

"I love the San Juan Capistrano station," Miranda said as she pointed to the historic area. "Before my mom died, we visited the mission together," she told him.

"When did your mom pass?" he asked. Passengers began boarding the train.

"Four years ago. It was always just the two of us. She died in a car accident on the Four-Oh-Five freeway."

"I'm so sorry, Miranda." He squeezed her hand. She gave him a small smile. "She was amazing."

"If she was anything like you, I imagine she was."

"We started out in Ohio. I don't remember a lot about it except for making snow men in the winters. She came out here for a better job."

"Where was your dad?"

"He was dead."

This time he took her hand in both of his, "That must have been really tough."

"He left before I was born. He was nothing to us. It was always just me and Mom."

Miranda loved the warm smile that he gave her. "So she came out here for a job? What kind?"

"She worked as a copywriter. It didn't pay a real lot, but it was enough for an apartment in a good neighborhood. She was the best, even when she was laid off when I was thirteen, she just went to night school to learn website design so she could start again. Nothing kept her down." Miranda sighed.

She remembered her Mom working days checking groceries and going to school at night and then coming home and doing her homework until one or two o'clock in the morning. It was up to her to make sure that the house was taken care of. Miranda didn't mind, considering everything her mom was doing. God, she missed her. She might have been twenty-four when her mother died, but she felt like a little girl when she got the news.

It was still so fresh, that moment when she received the call from Officer Gloria Vasquez of the California Highway Patrol. The woman's softly-accented voice would be forever burned into her memory. Miranda's first question had been if her mother had suffered, and the fact that Gloria couldn't immediately reassure her, had been heartbreaking.

Images of her mother, racked with pain, as she was pinned inside her crushed car still haunted Miranda.

Had her mom cried out for her?

She was so confused.

"Babe?"

Was that Griff's voice? Where was she?

"Mom?"

"No, Baby, wake up."

She felt Griff pull her close, right from the chair until his warm body surrounded her. She melted against him. She hiccupped a sob.

"That's it, let it out. I'm here for you."

That woke her up all the way. She burrowed her cheek into the crook of his neck, breathing in his scent, taking comfort, but doing everything in her power to gain control. One of his big hands sifted through her hair, another stroked down her back. She tried to jerk out of his arms, not wanting to need comfort.

"It's okay to cry you know."

"I know." Her breath echoed moist air back against her lips, and she tasted his skin.

"Miranda, Honey, talk to me," he coaxed.

She sighed. He probably wasn't going to let it go. Maybe that was a good thing.

"You were dreaming about your Mom?"

"I was dreaming about everything," she finally admitted. "It ended with my Mom."

"The train wreck, right?"

She hugged him tight, and then he rearranged them so that she was lying on top of him, his back resting against the arm of the big chair. It was perfect.

"Tell me," he cajoled gently.

"I shouldn't have to, you were there. It was hell. Anyway, we already talked about it."

"Did we?" He tipped her chin up forcing her to look him in the eye. "I answered your questions about what happened, but I never really told you how I felt. You never told me what was going on in your head, either."

She pulled her head away from his hold. "What was the point?"

"Baby, maybe it would help. I worry about you. Miranda, you get pretty wound up about this every year. You have nightmares."

"Griff they had every head doctor in the universe talk to me after the train wreck. I eventually got a clean bill of health, remember?"

Griff opened his mouth and then closed it.

"Say it. I won't bite your head off."

"Physically you got a clean bill of health, but Miranda, I know this eats at you. I just hate seeing you in pain. That's all."

Part of her lapped up his care and concern like a kitten with cream, and part of her wanted to rip his eyes out with her teeth. God, maybe she was crazy.

"So what are you saying?" she finally asked.

"Maybe it's time to lance the boil once and for all."

"Nice imagery, Porter," she tried to smirk, but her lower lip started to tremble, and she had to bite it. "What does that entail?"

"We talk more about that day, but include our feelings." He looked her dead in the eye. "We've talked about what happened, but we've never really discussed whether we were mad, or sad or scared."

"Wasn't that kind of obvious?"

God she hated this.

45

"Humor me," he brushed his knuckles over her cheek. "Tell you what, I'll start. You tell me where your dream left off."

"It was right before Josiah and Scarlett got on the train," she reluctantly answered.

Griff smiled. "It had sure been a surprise to see them." He shifted so that she could lie more comfortably on top of him. After they were comfortable, he began.

Three Years Earlier

"MA'AM, let me help you with that," a familiar voice said. Griff turned and saw his captain, Josiah Hale, and grinned. He had gone through BUD/S with the man's son, Nick Hale. He watched as the captain helped the older woman store her luggage over the lip of the upper metal rack above the seat. Betty saw Griff looking and winked. Josiah saw the wink and turned to look at Griff.

"Griff, is that you?"

Griff stood up and held out his hand. "Hello, Captain," he smiled easily as the man took his hand. He felt a tap on the shoulder and looked around. A graceful woman in her late forties smiled at him.

"Griffin Porter, the day just gets better and better," Scarlett Hale reached out for a hug that he gladly gave her. "It's almost like I have Nick here when I get to see someone from his class. We don't get out to the East Coast often enough to visit him," she said.

Griff looked into the warm brown eyes of a woman he had known for seven years. "Mrs. Hale, I can't wait to tell my mom that I saw you. She asks about you all the time."

"And how many times do I have to remind you to call me Scarlett?" She gave a good natured sigh.

"About as often as often as my mom has to remind Nick to call her Claudia," Griff grinned.

Josiah laughed as he brushed his fingertips along his wife's elbow and guided her to the seat across the aisle from Griff's and Miranda's. Griff could see the curious gleam in Scarlett's eye, but he also knew that she wouldn't be peppering Miranda with questions. That wasn't her style. He'd always been impressed by the Hales, and had been pleased when he learned that he would be serving a couple of levels under Captain Hale.

"Miranda, I'd like to introduce you to some old friends of mine. This is Captain Hale and his wife—"

"Scarlett," the older woman jumped in before Griff could call her Mrs. Hale. She held out her hand to Miranda.

"Scarlett is the mom of one of my best friends. He and I went through BUD/S together. He's serving on another team out in Virginia."

"It's very nice to meet you," Miranda smiled. "I'm Miranda Slade. I'm a project manager with TAID in San Diego. You arrived at the perfect time. I was just about ready to take Griff up on his offer to have dinner with him, but now that you've arrived you can act as a reference for him. Should I go out with him?"

Scarlett's eyes twinkled as she eyed Griff.

Oh Lord, what was she going to say? It was anyone's guess. She was as bad a tease as his own mother.

"Well, I have to tell you Miranda, I'm kind of biased. I'm married to a SEAL, and I raised one. These men are a breed unto themselves," her eyes twinkled.

"I'm beginning to agree with your assessment," Miranda said as she gave Griff a sideways look. He couldn't help but preen a little bit that she found him attractive. But Griff knew he was going to have to work on this, because Ms. Slade was awfully damn pretty herself and he'd had to guard his seat pretty zealously over the last two months.

When the train took a heavy lurch and she bumped into him, he took the opportunity to put his arm around her. Okay, he might be pushing things, but it was time. The moment that Griff waited to see what she would do was one of the longest of his life. For a second she looked startled, but then she smiled and snuggled into his side.

"I like this better than being on my phone," she whispered so just he could hear her.

"I don't know," Griff said. "You're pretty damn sexy when you're dressing down your subordinates."

"Dressing down. I like that. It sounds so militaristic. I should be wearing a uniform and carrying a riding crop like General Patton in that movie."

Griff almost groaned. Suddenly he had a picture of her in a leather dress and high-heeled lace-up boots.

Keep it together, Porter.

Miranda looked up at him and gave him a wicked smile. The vixen knew exactly what she'd done.

Thank God an announcement for another stop sounded over the speaker. Soon more people were coming on board, including a young mother with a toddler and a young child. She had all of the requisite child paraphernalia accompanying her.

Griff and Josiah both got out of their seats to assist her, which seemed to overwhelm both the woman and children. The little girl in her arms started to whimper, then as Griff offered to take the woman's suitcase, the little girl shrieked.

"No!"

"I'm so sorry," the young woman said. "Hope's going through the terrible twos."

Scarlett, seeing the problem, got out of her seat and stepped between the two men and the small family.

"I think those men are just too darn big, don't you, Hope?" Scarlett asked.

The small child took a moment to assess Scarlett. She seemed fascinated by her blue pendant. She stared at it and finally nodded her head, her brown curls bobbing around her face.

Scarlett turned to the mother. "My name is Scarlett Hale. The younger man is Griffin Porter and the other one is my husband Josiah. They're here to help with your things. Would it be okay if they stored some of your items in the overhead bin?"

Griff saw the overwhelming relief in the woman's eyes.

"My name's Susan." She juggled her little girl, then held out her hand to Scarlett as best she could. The older woman shook it, then Scarlett deftly took Susan's diaper bag and backpack. Nick's mom always could work miracles.

The little boy, no more than four years old, darted past the three adults. "Jeremy, come back here!" Susan yelled.

Griff watched as Miranda easily caught the kid and swooped him up into a high hug.

"Whatchya doing? Wanna come look out the window with me, Jeremy?"

His eyes widened with pleasure as he turned to his frazzled mother. "Yeah, can I Mom? Can I?" Miranda walked over with her little charge.

"Hi, I'm Miranda Slade," she said holding Jeremy.

Susan smiled around the other three adults in the aisle of the train. "I'm Susan. Thanks for catching my little monster."

"I'm not a monster. I'm Ironman," the boy chimed in.

Everyone but Miranda laughed.

"You look like Ironman," she said seriously. Then she turned to Susan. "It wasn't a problem," she said with a grin. "I played softball, I like a good game of catch. Can he come sit with me while you get settled with your daughter?"

"Are you sure?" the woman asked. Griff and Josiah let the women talk out the particulars as they put the luggage away.

"I'm positive," Miranda assured her.

"That'd be great."

Hope took that moment to let her presence be known as she started to wiggle in her mother's arms. "Want down," she whined.

"As a matter of fact, he can sit with me as long as he'd like. It's not a problem."

Griff sighed. Well, at least he'd gotten Miranda to agree to a date, and had the pleasure of her snuggling up against him.

"I don't want to be an inconvenience." Susan shifted Hope in her arms. The little girl looked at everyone with suspicious eyes again since she was being ignored. Then her stare shifted to Griff and suddenly, like the sun showing up after a thunderstorm, she smiled. "Hiya!"

All of the adults laughed and said 'Hello' or 'Hiya' back to Hope.

"I'm serious, I would love it if Jeremy sat with me," Miranda reiterated.

"I wanna sit with Mira, Mom," Jeremy piped up.

"How'd you know my nickname?" Miranda asked the little boy. "That's what the kids at school used to call me. You're pretty smart."

He giggled as she gently poked his tummy. She turned and started walking back to her seat.

The train started again. "Susan, would you like a cup of coffee? I'm going to send the men for refreshments," Scarlett said.

"You are?" Josiah said with amusement as he stroked his hand down his wife's straight, blond hair.

"Yep. Miranda, what would you like to drink?" Scarlett called out to her.

"I'd kill for a cup of coffee. Jeremy, would you like apple or orange juice?" Miranda asked.

"Grape. Where are they going? Mommy, can I go with them?" He wiggled to be let out of Miranda's arms. She let him down.

"You can't go with them. You have to stay on this car with us," Susan said. Griff watched as the boy's face scrunched up.

"Susan, how about we show him how the automatic door works between the railroad cars, then have him go sit back with Miranda? He could even press the button to open the door," Griff suggested.

"Can I Mom? Can I?" Jeremy asked in a familiar refrain as he bounced on his feet.

Susan shot Griff a grateful smile. "Sure, they'll show you, but then you go right back to Miranda," she admonished.

"Okay, Mommy." He grabbed Griff's hand and started tugging him toward the back of the car. He and Josiah grinned at one another, reveling in the child's enthusiasm.

"Hold on, Partner. We need to ask your mom what she would like to drink," Josiah told the boy. Griff watched as Susan fumbled for her purse.

"I've got this," Josiah assured her. "What would you like?"

"But—"

Griff watched as his captain just raised an authoritative eyebrow. That, along with a warm smile, had Susan giving him a grateful look. "Milk for Hope, and I'd like an orange juice. Thank you."

"Got it."

"And I know what *you* want." Josiah gave his wife a devilish smile, and Griff watched as Scarlett's cheeks warmed.

Damn, that man had it going on.

Griff turned to Miranda. "How do you like your coffee?"

"Pitch black."

"Are you sure you weren't in the Navy?" he asked.

Miranda laughed.

Griff liked that she didn't try to offer any money. It was as if she were aware that their relationship had changed since she had agreed to go out with him. Jeremy tugged on his hand again, and he started down the aisle with Josiah following him. As they got to the back of the railroad car, there was a spot where they could go down the stairs. "Do we go down there?" Jeremy asked.

"Nope, that's where you go when you want to get on and off the train," Josiah said. He pointed to the door at the end of the car. "Press that button. You have to press really hard, little man." The boy used both hands, and eventually it opened to the small passageway between the two railcars.

"You did it Jeremy!" Josiah crouched down and held out his palm. "High five."

"Now what?" Jeremy asked after slapping Josiah's huge hand with his little one.

"Now Griff and I are going to go through the next

door to the other car and go down the stairs to the café and get the drinks. We'll be right back."

"Can I go with you? Please?" the boy wheedled.

"Nope, you have to be a good boy and go back to Miranda like you promised you would." Josiah stood up, and pointed back to where the women were standing. Jeremy reluctantly started walking back.

"Cute kid," Griff said.

"He's a handful. Reminds me of Nick at that age. Always pushing his limits. Of course not nearly as bad as Gianna. Now that girl ran roughshod over everyone but her mother."

Griff thought of Nick's baby sister. Yep, she was the spitting image of Scarlett. Nick swore he had started to sport gray hairs at twenty-four because of his baby sister.

"How is your daughter doing?" he asked Josiah as they walked through the passageway to the next car. It was quieter than the one they were staying in.

"Gianna got an internship at a design firm in D.C. They have her making coffee, and occasionally she gets to work with something called mood boards." Josiah rolled his eyes. "The coffee I understand, but the mood boards escape me. She's pretty damned excited, though. At least it's interior design and not fashion."

"I don't know, I could see Gianna taking the fashion world by storm."

Josiah shuddered. "Next thing you know she'd be making friends with models and Nick would be dropping out of the Navy. No thank you."

Griff laughed. The captain had a point. They

made their way downstairs and found four commuters in line ahead of them. Griff gathered the drinks for the kids, then poured two coffees into paper cups.

"Let me pay for Susan's stuff," Josiah said.

"No, I've got it." Griff already had his wallet out.

Josiah nodded, then he picked up some Cheerios and bananas. Griff just grinned at his captain. The man was a serious soft touch.

Griff leaned against one of the high tables as Josiah doctored his wife's coffee.

"So you met Miranda on the train?" Josiah asked.

"Yep, we've been commuting together every Monday for the last nine weeks. I finally asked her to go out with me this morning."

"You're moving kind of slow, aren't you?" Josiah said as he set down the container of creamer. Then Josiah's gaze pierced him. "Damn, Griff, I'm the one who's slow today. You're commuting in from your parents', aren't you?"

Griff nodded.

"Nick mentioned something last year about your dad being ill, but he didn't say anything again, so I thought he was fine. What's going on?"

"Dad's going through chemo. But things are really looking up now. It's been tough on my mom, and Darla is pregnant with her first baby, so there's a lot going on. I've been trying to give Dad and Mom as much of my time as possible."

Josiah clapped him on his shoulder. "You're doing good, Son."

"What about you? Why are you and Scarlett on the train?"

"We did the bed and breakfast thing in San Juan Capistrano."

Looking out the window over the ocean, Griff suddenly had a vision of Miranda lying in a four poster bed. She'd look beautiful with her black hair fanned out over a pillow.

"Are you with me, Porter?" Josiah asked with a shit-eating grin.

"Sorry, my brain just got side-tracked for a—"

A thunderous roar.

The train lurched.

As if in slow motion, Griff saw the coffee begin to rise as his body was propelled up off the floor. He was thrown up and backwards, like he was in a tidal wave.

The lights went out, but the sun still shone through cracked and broken windows.

He heard the metal shriek.

His head and back slammed into steel.

Everything went dark.

GRIFF PAUSED for a long time in his telling of the story, then he kissed Miranda softly on her forehead. "I've never been more scared in my life, than when I woke up. All I thought about was getting back to you. I couldn't believe that the crash could have happened while Josiah and I were away from our two women."

"So, you had already considered me 'your woman'?" Miranda questioned with a hint of laughter.

"Oh, Baby, you might not have known it, but you'd been mine for weeks." Again he looked deep into her eyes. "And for you? What was it like when you woke up?"

4
————

MIRANDA SWALLOWED. SHE'D NEVER REALLY TOLD GRIFF all that had gone on with her. Part of it had been that she'd had a tough time remembering everything after the wreck. But when her memories had resurfaced, her natural inclination was to keep things to herself.

"I really want to know. Not just what happened, I want to know how you felt. It's time." How could his voice be both firm and coaxing? But he was right. It was time.

———

THREE YEARS Earlier

MIRANDA WOKE UP TO DARKNESS. Something was wriggling underneath her belly, and something hard and heavy was pressing against her leg, and God, did it hurt. Everything hurt. What the hell had happened?

She tasted copper. Her mouth was full of blood. She opened it and let it drip out. Then her ears popped and that's when she heard loud metallic groaning. This was some bad shit.

"Mommy! I want my Mommy!" The wriggling turned to kicking.

Train. She was on the train. There'd been a crash. The wriggling was the little boy who'd been sitting on her lap.

The angry little voice turned tearful. "Where's my Mommy?"

Miranda tried to answer. The little legs packed a punch, the kicks hurt. She could move her arms, and she tried to stop the blows, but something was blocking her. Why was it so dark? She spit out some more blood before she gagged.

"Jeremy," she croaked.

"Mommy!" came the frantic cry.

"Honey, we'll find your mommy." Miranda thought about moving off the boy, but she didn't want him to scramble away. Why was it so dark? Hadn't it been late morning? Had she been unconscious for hours? Was it night? It didn't make sense, rescue workers would have been here by now if it were night.

She turned her head and saw that a seat was covering her. Her shoulders were blocked by the arms of the seat, and something was pressing down on her right leg. She tried to move it and the pain made the darkness turn to red. "Mother—" she bit off the foul curse.

"Mommy?" the boy asked again.

"No, I don't see your mommy yet. Jeremy, are you hurt?"

"My arm hurts."

The boy started to cry. Shit, she shouldn't have asked, now he was focused on what was hurting. Miranda tried to expand her scope of hearing, listening for all she was worth to see if there was anybody else alive.

"Derek, wake up! Wake up!" The woman's shrill voice was far away. She kept repeating the same words over and over again, until finally she subsided into sobs. It drove home the fact that she and Jeremy were lucky to be alive.

She needed to figure out what was on her leg and get moving. It wasn't the seat, so what was it? She wiggled her shoulders and was finally able to touch the leather of her computer bag. She shoved her hand in and found her cell phone. She powered it on, and dialed nine-one-one.

"What's the nature of your emergency?"

"I'm on the Amtrak train heading to San Diego. We've crashed outside of Del Mar."

"We know, first responders are on their way. What is your name?"

"Miranda Slade."

"Can you tell me where you are? What is your situation?"

"I want my Mommy." Jeremy grabbed at her phone and knocked it out of her hands.

Shit.

Miranda picked it up and heard, "Ma'am. Miranda. Can you describe what is going on?"

"Look, just get help," Miranda said. "I'm going to use the flashlight on the phone to figure out how to get unstuck. I'll call back when I can." Miranda disconnected while the woman was talking.

She shone the light on Jeremy. His little face was streaked with tears. He didn't seem to be bleeding anywhere, thank the Lord. Miranda was pretty sure she had some loose teeth and her jaw hurt like a son of a bitch. She shone the light on her leg. It looked like part of a luggage rack was wedged on top of her thigh. She tried to lift it, but the seat was on top of it.

"Miranda?" She heard a weak cry.

"Scarlett?"

Nothing.

"Scarlett."

"Please. Mira. I want my Mom." The little boy sounded desolate. He was killing her. Miranda had to get her leg free so that she could go look for the two women and baby Hope. If Jeremy wriggled free he would go wandering, she just knew it.

"We'll find your mommy, I promise, Jeremy."

How was she going to get free?

"Does anybody need help?" A man's voice yelled from a distance.

Miranda almost shouted out Griff's name, until her brain clued into the fact it wasn't his voice.

"Me! Help me." Another man cried out.

She heard glass breaking.

"Holy fuck! We're going to fall onto the beach." A different man's voice said.

Miranda vaguely remembered that she had been staring at a beautiful view of the ocean and that they had been near a good-sized drop-off. Please say they weren't near that spot.

The screech of steel vibrated down her spine. Fear pierced her brain.

"Don't move!" the same man's voice yelled out.

Screams shattered the darkness.

She had to get her leg unstuck. She had to. Miranda yanked, then bit her lip in excruciating pain. Teeth. Jaw. Lip. Leg. She let out a watery sob.

Keep it together, Slade. There's no crying in baseball. Think. Think.

She needed leverage to lift the luggage rack. Finally, her brain kicked into gear. She dragged her computer case over to her, and turned it so that the wheels faced her. She positioned the edge under the rack. Using the case as a wedge and shoving with all her strength, the rack eventually began to lift. Miranda pulled her leg out, ignoring the pain. At least this time, she didn't bite her lip.

As soon as her leg came free, so did Jeremy.

Dammit.

He was up like a shot. "Wait!" Her chin hit the floor as she lunged uselessly. He was slippery as an eel, and now she tasted blood *and* snot.

"Come back," she choked. Miranda dragged herself out from under the seat. At long last, she was back out into the very dim light of the train car. She saw the light of her phone and snatched it up. She shone it around and gasped at the devastation surrounding her.

The train was on its side. Seats were torn from their moorings and scattered against the shattered windows on the floor. No, wait, that was the side of the train. She shook her head, trying to orient herself. The side of the train was now the floor. She was standing on glass. She needed her shoes, fast. When she whipped her head around to look, she got dizzy and her head hurt.

Suck it up.

She saw one pump on the floor, and then the other. She slipped them on.

"Lady?" She saw a man sitting, holding his arm that had an obvious compound fracture. He was bleeding heavily from his scalp.

"I have to find the little boy who must have just run by you. Did you see which way he went?"

He tipped his head, indicating he went behind her.

"Thank you."

Miranda still wasn't sure which way Susan and Scarlett were, based on how the train was now situated.

"Scarlett? Susan? Jeremy?"

No answer.

She'd try for a Mom voice.

"Jeremy! Young Man! You answer me right this minute!"

"I'm here."

Miranda slumped in relief. She saw a flash of green and realized it was his shirt. He was waving. She climbed over two seats, scrunching her toes so her shoes stayed on.

He was looking down. Oh God, it was a dead body. She picked him up.

"What's wrong with her?"

"She's sleeping, Honey."

Please God, let his mom and sister be all right. "Susan!" she yelled out. "Scarlett!"

"Over here." She heard a weak voice. It was Scarlett's.

The voice came from in front of her. She could have sworn Scarlett would have been behind her and closer to where she had been sitting. Her sense of direction was all off. Miranda took a step in the direction of the voice, doing her best to keep hold of Jeremy. At least he was doing a monkey hold, with his legs wrapped around her waist and his arms around her neck.

The train lurched and she slipped and landed hard. She hit her hip on one of the overturned seats. The pain reverberated up her leg, but Jeremy hung on tight. Neither of them hit the floor. She heard more screams.

"We're going to die!" It was a woman's voice.

Did Miranda hear a siren?

Sea grass peeked through some broken glass. Instead of darkness from the window below her, she could see a sliver of light. Miranda fought back a wave of nausea because when she squinted, she could see the sandy beach at least a hundred feet below.

The train car was literally perched on the edge of the cliff. They would die if the train plummeted over the side of the cliff.

"Jeremy? Hope?" It was Susan's voice.

Stop focusing on the beach.

She clutched Jeremy tighter as he tried to squirm out of her arms.

"Mommy! I'm here." He hit her shoulder. "Let me down, Mira."

"Hold on, Honey. Let me take you to your mother. It's not safe for you to be walking around in the dark. There's glass everywhere." Miranda struggled to stand upright, but she finally managed to get her feet under her.

Dammit, she was missing a shoe again. She felt around with her toe, while still dealing with a stubborn little boy who was determined to get away from her.

"Please Jeremy, hold still. I need you to hang on like the little monkey I know you can be. Your mommy might be stuck like we were, and we have to get to her together."

"Really?"

"Yes, really," she choked out as he all but strangled her.

Eureka, she found her shoe. Why in the hell had she worn heels? But at least she hadn't cut her feet...yet. Glass crunched under her feet as she moved.

"Susan? Call out. We're coming."

"Do you have Jeremy and Hope?"

Miranda's heart broke at the thought of the little girl being away from her mother.

"I have Jeremy. Maybe Hope is with Scarlett. Keep talking to me."

"I'm here," came the reply. It was closer. Miranda maneuvered past sheet metal and insulation. She looked up and saw that some of the siding had come off the wall along with the luggage racks. The steel had sharp edges and she had to be careful as she went around it to get to Susan.

As she stepped over somebody's suitcase, her leg gave out. Miranda dropped down to one knee.

"Mira?" Jeremy's voice quavered.

"It's okay, Sweets. We're almost to your mom."

Miranda reached out to grab ahold of one of the seats to help herself up, even though her leg didn't want to cooperate.

"Come on, Slade, we don't have time for this shit," she said under her breath.

Jeremy cupped her cheeks and looked her in the eye. "You said a bad word."

"I'm sorry." She grit her teeth, which was a mistake. She was going to need a dentist for sure. She pushed herself up.

Just a couple more steps.

Come on.

Just a couple more steps.

She found Susan.

Miranda didn't know if she felt like crying with relief or worry, because Susan looked like she'd been in a train wreck. She stifled a hysterical laugh. But seriously, Susan looked like hell. Her once-blond hair was matted with blood and her leg was at an odd angle.

"Jeremy." Had Miranda ever heard so much love contained in one word?

"Mommy."

Susan stretched her arms out to her son, but Miranda didn't hand him over.

"Susan, how bad is your head?" Miranda asked quietly, not wanting to alarm Jeremy. She bent down so that mom and son could at least hug.

Tear-stained eyes looked up at her. "I think it's bad. I keep going in and out of consciousness. But it just might be from the pain."

"Jeremy, I'll let you down," Miranda told the little boy. "But you have to be extra gentle with your mom. She's hurting. You can't jostle her, okay?"

He gave her a confused look.

"You can't play rough with her," she explained.

"She's hurted?"

"Her leg and her head hurt." Miranda looked at Susan, whose eyes were closed. "You have to be gentle and take good care of her. Can you do that?" She set him down beside his mother and he pressed against his mother softly. He stroked her arm gently.

"Mommy, can you hear me?"

Susan's eyes opened. "I can hear you just fine, Baby."

"Are you hurted?"

"Not now that you're here." She moved her arm and snuggled him close. Susan had her backpack next to her. She fumbled with it. Miranda helped her pull out a sweatshirt for Jeremy to sit on.

"When was the last time you saw Hope?" Miranda asked.

"I don't know. When I woke up, she was gone. I couldn't go look for her. I've called out a couple of times when I heard people, but nobody has come by to help until you." Then Susan did a head tilt toward the crumpled seat to her left. For the first time Miranda noted that a baby blanket was covering something. Now that she looked, she realized that Susan must have covered a body with Hope's blanket.

"I would have kept calling, but it hurts to yell. Then I heard you calling out for me, so I called back. Thank God you had Jeremy." She reached out and clutched Miranda's wrist. "Can you find Hope?"

"Of course." She'd also try to find Scarlett. She prayed that the two of them were together and healthy.

Please, God, let them be safe.

Please, God.

IT TOOK a moment for Miranda to realize she wasn't on the train. Instead, she was in her living room in San Diego three years later with Griff holding her so tight that she was having trouble breathing.

"Jesus, Miranda, I never knew." Griff was actually trembling.

"Hey," she crooned. "It wasn't that bad."

He sat up, taking her with him. "What the fuck do you mean it wasn't that bad? It was a fucking nightmare."

She pressed her hand against his lips. "Griffin, we got through this."

Her breath caught when she saw the sheen of wet on his brown eyes.

"It was so close. So close. I almost lost you."

His fingers tangled in her hair and he tilted her head.

His lips slammed down on hers. He devoured her. In their three years together, he had never kissed her with such need. Such intensity. It was as if his life depended on it. Miranda's nails clawed at his shoulders. His mouth bit at hers, possessing her body, ruling her soul.

Miranda capitulated. His dominion soothed her, it let her know that in this moment she didn't have to be in control, that she could entirely trust someone else to take care of everything.

Griff ripped off her sleepshirt, flinging it over the side of the chair. He ripped her lace panties. Actually *ripped* them off her body. A thrill raced down her spine.

Miranda whimpered her need.

Griff's head whipped up, his eyes seeking hers. "You with me?"

"I need you," she ground out hoarsely.

He waited a beat.

"Now," she demanded. "I need you, now."

"You can never as much as I need you." His hands were everywhere, touching, caressing, setting her skin on fire. He slipped to the carpet and he stroked his hot hands up the insides of her legs, stretching her wide.

"Beautiful." His voice was guttural.

She believed him. He parted her flesh with his thumbs, and feasted.

Miranda grabbed for the back of the chair, but she missed, her hands flailing uselessly as spirals of heat and passion hurtled through her body. How was this even possible?

Griffin was relentless. Every stab of his tongue

touched off another jolt of sensation that had her crying his name. She was frantic with want, but as he adjusted his hold, pulling her closer, she heard him.

"Mine."

Her face was wet, her head whipped back and forth, her hair sticking to her tears.

"Mine."

He rose up and jerked down his sweatpants. She looked up greedily. At last, something to hold onto. She tried to touch his cock, but he grabbed her wrists in one hand, and looked down with an intense smile.

"Do you trust me?" he asked.

"With my life."

He guided himself to her entrance and thrust home.

She moaned her pleasure, wrapping her legs around him. Biting his shoulder, hard. Too hard.

Never had it been like this. She looked up at the man she loved and barely recognized his face. "Griff," she gasped out.

"It's okay, I'm here. We made it.

"Mine." He swooped down and laid claim to her mouth. She opened, welcoming, taking him into her body. She knew that Griff needed to feel, needed to believe that she was here, that she was whole and his.

She broke their kiss, wrestled her hands from his grasp, and cupped his cheeks. "I'm going to be here. Always, Griff. Always."

He surged high inside her, and Miranda about lost her mind.

"You can't leave me. I couldn't live without you," he whispered.

"You won't have to," she breathed against his mouth.

His strokes changed, gifting her with pleasure. Her head rolled side to side. It was too much.

Griff bent his head and curled his tongue around her nipple, then suckled as he drove her even higher.

"Now," she begged.

His dark eyes glimmered with a hint of a smile. "Patience is a virtue."

"Fuck virtue," she cried.

He laughed.

Thank God, he was her Griffin again. She wrapped her arms around his shoulders and arched against him, then gently bit the pulse in his neck as he gently bit down on her nipple.

Ecstasy.

5
_____

"GRIFF, YOU DON'T HAVE TO DO THIS," MIRANDA laughed.

It amazed him that after this long together, his wife could still be self-conscious around him. He could mention the fact that he'd been in the delivery room with her, but he wasn't a foolish man.

"Hush, this gives me pleasure," he said, as he stroked the wash cloth down her pale skin. God, her beauty blew him away. It always had.

"You're the one who said she didn't want to get her hair wet in the shower," he reminded her.

"You know the blow dryer always wakes Livvie up."

Griff loved the way she arched into the warm cloth. When he was done he blotted her with one of their new, soft bath towels.

"Okay, Missy, it's way past your bedtime. Let's get you under the covers."

When they were under the comforter, he pulled her into his arms and tried to blot out what she had told him. How come he wasn't surprised when she gave him that look?

"Okay, I told you mine, now it's time for you to tell me yours."

"I have," he said, trying to shut down any more talk of the train wreck. It would take a long time for her words to work their way out of his system.

"Griffin, I told you how it was for me. It's only fair that you return the favor. I vaguely remember you telling me about it after the fact, but now I want to really know. What happened? How was it actually?"

"Well, I told you that all I could think about was you and getting to you. I was with Josiah, and his need to get back to Scarlett was just as bad. It was like looking in a mirror. I've been on some hairy fucking missions, but nothing, not one damn thing, has scared me like that day."

Three Years Earlier

"Josiah, can you hear me?" Griff shook the older man. Except for the cut on his arm, he looked okay.

Josiah Hale's eyes popped open. "We crashed?"

"Affirmative." Griff breathed easier, seeing that his Captain, a fellow SEAL, was going to be working with him.

"How bad?" Josiah asked.

"Bad. We're right outside of Del Mar, beside the

cliffs overlooking the ocean. This car is leaning over. When I looked out the window, I could see the car with the women was on its side, and it doesn't look stable."

"How not stable?" Josiah bit out the question.

"Can't tell from here. Worst case? It'll take a hundred foot drop at any minute."

Just saying it made bile rise in Griff's mouth.

"Do you know why we crashed?" Josiah pushed himself off the floor, giving a quick glance to his arm. Griff thrust a towel that he'd found from the café at Josiah so that he could staunch the bleeding.

"We were going too fucking slow for it to cause something this bad. It's got to be an explosion. We could have unfriendlies," Griff said grimly.

"Fuck."

Josiah pulled out his phone and pressed a number on his speed dial. He waited.

He looked at Griff. "She's not answering."

He placed another call.

"Liam, I have a situation." His voice was calm and commanding. "Amtrak train crashed heading south to San Diego outside Del Mar. I'm on it with Scarlett, she's in another car that could fall into the ocean. It's going to be a cluster for the emergency workers to get to us, we're not near a highway." He looked for Griff for confirmation.

Griff nodded.

"Which teams are in-country?" Josiah asked.

Griff watched the older man squint as he listened. "Have Mason and Gray get their men here, stat. Also see about help from Camp Pendleton. If I don't answer," he finally said, "text me." Then he hung up.

Griff felt a hell of a lot better knowing that Lieutenant Commander Liam McAllister was on point to gather up his SEAL team and another one. He knew that the men on his team could work miracles.

As one unit, Griff and Josiah turned and surveyed the interior of the café car. There were five people other than themselves inside. One commuter was already helping a woman. They looked like they were going to be fine. The older Vietnamese gentleman who ran the diner was currently trying to apply pressure to another man's arm to stop the river of bleeding coming from his deltoid. The last passenger in the car was a woman lying against the wall. She didn't look injured. Josiah veered off to the bleeding man, Griff crouched down next to the woman.

"Are you okay, Ma'am?"

"Did we crash?" she asked softly. Her brown eyes were wet with tears.

"Yes, are you okay?"

"Can you get me off the train? I want to get off the train." She gripped Griff's arm.

"Ma'am, I need you to remain calm. Help is on the way." He'd already called nine-one-one, as had many others, according to the operator.

"Ma'am, do you have your phone?"

She grabbed her purse and pulled out her phone, then she nodded.

"Why don't you call your family and tell them that you're all right?" he suggested. "My friend and I are going to go look for other people who are injured, okay?"

She wasn't paying him any attention, she was already dialing. He looked over his shoulder at Josiah. It looked like things were under control. Good. They needed to get to the car where the women were. There was no exit on the bottom level of the dining car like there had been on the one the women were on. If they wanted to get to the women, they would need to go upstairs and go through the passageway. But when he checked the electrical, it wasn't working.

"We need to climb out the window," Griff said to Josiah. He pointed to the big window that overlooked the ocean. It was severely cracked, and even though it was made of safety glass, there was a hole in the bottom left hand corner where a piece had broken out.

"People, I need you to move away from the window," Josiah yelled as he strode over to the jumbled mess that had once been the café. He picked up the sturdy steel microwave off the floor and yanked the plug out of the wall socket. He took aim, and hurled it close to the hole in the window. It crashed through, bringing in the fresh ocean air.

The woman who had been talking on her phone screamed. "What are you doing?"

"Ma'am, we need to get out to help the people in the other car," Josiah calmly answered.

Without being asked, the man who ran the diner was beside Griff with a handful of towels. "Here, put these down over the glass so you don't cut yourselves when you climb out."

"No need," Griff said. "This is safety glass." He pushed the entire remaining piece out of its moorings in one big chunk. He climbed out first and was surprised to see two lanky young men in wet suits making their way up over the rise of the cliff. It took a brief second for it to register with him that they had probably been surfing when they had heard or seen the crash.

"Hey, are you okay?" The first kid was a blond who couldn't be more than fifteen or sixteen.

"Yeah," Josiah answered. "We're headed over to that car."

Griff stared at where the captain was pointing and really took his first good look.

His stomach dropped.

"There was definitely an explosion," Josiah said. Griff saw smoke coming from the two cars farther up the track, but the one that he was interested in was on its side. Part of it had been sheared off like someone had taken a gigantic can opener to it, but the thing that scared the shit out of him was that it was literally teetering on the edge of the cliff. It was easily a hundred-foot drop, and if it fell to the sand below, there probably wouldn't be any survivors.

Griff and Josiah started toward the railroad car.

"Mister, don't you want to wait for the emergency workers? They should be here soon, we called them," one of the kids yelled after them.

Griff knew that it was going to be complicated for the first responders to get to this area because it was not accessible by road. Josiah had done the exact right thing by calling in the SEAL teams.

"My wife is on that train," Josiah said, never breaking stride.

As they got closer, Griff perused the metal wreckage.

"What do you think?" Josiah asked.

As soon as the question was out of his mouth, a chunk of sandy cliff broke away from underneath the weight of the passenger car, causing it to shift a little more toward the ocean. Griff winced when he heard the faint sound of screams from inside. But he knew damn good and well there wasn't a chance in hell it was Miranda or Scarlett who were screaming. Those two women were keeping their shit together.

He eyed Josiah. He nodded in silent agreement as he read Griff's mind. Yep, they knew their women.

"If we go underneath and try to climb through a window, the train could shift again and we'd be flatter than a pancake." Griff stated the obvious as they arrived at their destination.

Josiah nodded and grabbed a handhold on the back of the railcar and started climbing. Griff followed. Soon they were on top of the damaged car, which was actually the side. From that vantage point, they could see an opening near the back. It was small, but they should be able to work their way in.

Should.

"We need to stay near the edge, away from the cliff side," Griff said. They were in mission mode, so ensuring that nothing was assumed was part standard operating procedure. Josiah nodded at his words.

They made their way swiftly to the far edge. Griff felt sweat trickling down his back. When they got to the opening, Griff wondered how in the hell they were going to fit. Not only was it a tight fit, the steel was knife-sharp.

Josiah pulled out his phone and deployed the flashlight feature, then peered inside. "Looks like a three to four meter drop, but the seats have unbolted so it'll be a lousy landing." Griff looked over his captain's shoulder, scouting the terrain.

"Are you seeing what I'm seeing?" Josiah asked.

Griff nodded grimly. There were three people lying in the wreckage. It was clear that two of them were dead. One might still be alive. This was the upper deck of the train, business class, where they had all been seated. But according to Griff's calculations, they had left the women on the other end.

Griff peeled off his jacket and placed it over the edge of the steel so that maybe they wouldn't cut themselves on at least one of the sides of the hole. "I'll go first," Griff said. "You can lower me down. I'll move what I can, so it's a better landing when I help you down."

"Affirmative," Josiah answered.

"Hey."

Griff and Josiah's heads swivelled. One of the surfer's heads popped up where they had climbed over. He easily swung himself up and looked around, walking on the far side of the car, and swiftly made his way over to them. "I thought you could use this." He thrust out his hand.

Griff recognized it immediately. It was a surfboard leash that the surfers used to connect their feet to their boards so that when they crashed, so they didn't have to searching for their surfboards.

"Perfect, thanks."

"I called my brother, he and some of his teammates are coming from Coronado to help."

Griff looked closely at the young man as he wrapped the cord around his wrist, but he didn't recognize him. "Who's your brother?"

"Mason Gault."

"Small world," Josiah whistled as he looked up from where he was crouched. "Your brother's a good man. What's your name?"

"I'm Billy Anderson," the teenager replied.

Josiah stood up. "I'm Captain Hale, this is Griff Porter, he's on the Black Dawn team."

"Doesn't Mase work for you?" Billy asked.

"Yep," Josiah nodded.

Griff handed the end of the leash to Josiah, then sat down on the edge of the hole. It was going to be tight.

"Griff?" Billy said.

Griff looked up at the kid and raised his eyebrow in question.

"Maybe I should go down. I'd fit easier."

"No." Griff and Josiah said in unison.

"You're going to help me lower Griff down into the opening. Then, when the others arrive, you're going to direct them to this opening. Got it?" Josiah said.

Billy nodded.

It was a tight fit. But Griff worked his way through the hole and the leash ended about six feet above one of the upended seats. He easily dropped down, and as soon as he was clear of the wreckage, he unwrapped the cord and Josiah pulled it up.

Griff used his phone flash light to start checking things out. His first order of business was to check on the woman that he'd been hoping was alive. She wasn't.

He waited for Josiah to come down. He knew that Billy wouldn't be able to hold his weight, so Griff was ready to assist the man on his descent. But there was no need. Josiah dropped down with catlike reflexes and both men turned around and called out.

"Scarlett?"

"Miranda?"

"Griff?" Miranda responded.

Josiah called out his wife's name again. When there wasn't a response, Griff could almost feel his fear.

"Are you all right, Miranda?" Griff shouted.

"I am. Susan's injured, and I haven't found Scarlett or Hope."

"We're coming," Josiah said.

"Help," a man's weak voice came from their right.

"We'll be there," Griff responded. Josiah and he worked together to move a seat out of the way, as well as a luggage rack and some duffle bags and suitcases.

"Guys, do you see the light on the ceiling?" Miranda shouted out.

"Yes," Griff responded as he looked up. It was a

rotating circle of light about fifteen meters ahead of them. His girl was smart.

"Scarlett," Josiah called out again. Still no answer. Then he called again, his booming voice filled the entire car. "Scarlett Anne, answer me."

Again, he was met by a moment of silence, but then a cacophony of voices raised. A chorus of people calling for help. Griff and Josiah looked at one another, knowing that they were needed. Griff felt for his friend's father, knowing that his first priority was to find his wife.

As they started forward, there was a thud behind them. When he turned, Griff saw Billy.

"I told you not to come down here," Josiah all but roared. "You needed to tell people where we were." Griff winced, it was the first time he had heard his captain come down so harshly on someone.

"There's a helicopter hovering up there. He saw me, and knows I went inside. Look, I can help. I've taken first aid classes." Griff was impressed at how well the kid held up against Josiah, but all that changed when he had to step around a dead body. Griff and Josiah waited and it didn't take long for Billy to straighten up and look at them. "Seriously," he said in a low voice. "I can help."

Griff was impressed.

"In that case, follow us. And be careful where you step," Josiah said.

They all forged forward, when a hand raised up behind the next seat they came across.

"Can you help me up?"

Josiah carefully pulled an older African American man to his feet.

"Are you okay, Sir?"

"I'm in one piece. I just need a few minutes to catch my breath, then I can help. The train's slipping, right?" He looked between Josiah and Griff.

They both nodded.

"Well, let's start evacuating," he said briskly.

"Maybe you should rest a little longer," Griff suggested.

"Bullshit. We're burning daylight. Let's get going."

Griff figured it had been fifteen minutes since the crash happened. They were maybe three miles outside of Del Mar. Rescue workers should be on-site at any moment. As if his mind had conjured it, he heard the faint sound of sirens, hopefully they had figured out a way to get close to the train over the embankments. Except for maybe the Serrano Valley, he didn't know of any place worse that the crash could have happened.

The four males moved slowly and carefully forward, they didn't want to miss anyone as they made their way to Miranda and hopefully Scarlett.

"Please, my husband needs help," a woman called from the left. Josiah flashed his light over an older couple huddled near the side of the train. She was holding her coat against a wound on the man's belly.

"Billy, open some luggage and find something to staunch the bleeding," Griff ordered.

Griff looked at Josiah, who was hesitating. "I've got this, you go on ahead."

84

"Thanks," the big man said as he continued forward to look for his missing wife.

"Will this work?" Billy was holding up a flannel shirt that he was already beginning to tear into strips. He also had a sweatshirt in his hands. Griff was really liking the kid, he seriously had his shit together.

As they knelt down beside the injured man, Billy leaned in to whisper to Griff, "Should we pull out the metal?" he asked.

Griff examined it. "No, it will just cause more bleeding. Put the compresses around it."

The train gave a slow lurch and steel screeched.

The woman bit back a sob, but then looked at Griff clear-eyed. "What do I need to do? I know you need to help others."

His heart ached for her, even as he appreciated her bravery.

"There's a helicopter above us," Billy said. "I saw them. There's going to be EMT's real soon," Billy assured the woman.

Griff put his fingers to the man's neck again. His pulse was stronger.

Pounding on the outside wall of the train made the lady jump and the wounded man's eyelids flicker. Cries echoed inside as people jolted in fear. Griff yelled out. "Ladies and Gentlemen, please calm down. That's the sound of the rescue workers outside. They're just getting things in place to help us out."

Lord, he hoped he wasn't lying.

He gripped Billy's shoulder. "Call your brother. Find out his ETA."

Griff pulled out his phone at the same time. It was about damn time he checked in with his team. As soon as he did, he grinned. He had a text. It was from his team's crazy ass techie. Black Dawn had been together for less than a year, and they were just getting to know one another, but Griff really liked Dex Evans. The man seemed to know what everybody needed before they needed it.

Apparently, Griff had missed five calls in the last seventeen minutes. Dex had sent a long diatribe of a text, that told him the exact ETA of the Black Dawn team.

"Mason, where are you?" The kid put his phone on speaker.

"We're four-wheeling past Jaden's van toward the train tracks. We've spotted the helicopter. Fuck, Billy, we can see smoke. You're not near the train, are you?"

Billy didn't answer, and Griff took the phone from him.

"Mason? This is Griffin Porter. I'm with Black Dawn. Your brother is in the train even though our Captain Hale forbade him to enter it. Right now, your brother is providing aid to the injured and doing a damn fine job. The car we're on is on its side and near the cliff. I won't lie, it's not good. We need equipment to make sure it doesn't slip over the cliff."

"You need to evacuate," Mason said, his voice terse.

"Agreed, but it's a mess. We've barely found a quarter of the passengers on the top floor, and we haven't even made it to the bottom floor. It was the morning commute." Somebody was talking near

Mason, but Griff couldn't make out what they were saying. "So how close are you?" Griff asked.

"I've surfed the beach where Billy was, we should be there in five more minutes. There's another truck behind us. They've been tailing us since we left Coronado. Now that you said you're Black Dawn and the Captain is with you, chances are it's your teammates or some guys that Commander McAllister has pulled in."

Griff felt a burst of hope for the first time since the crash had occurred. He knew of Mason's Midnight Delta team because one of his teammates was now working with Mason's guys. Between Mason's team and Black Dawn, he was finally beginning to feel some hope.

6

MIRANDA AND GRIFF RAISED THEIR HEADS AS THEY heard Livvie's cry through the baby monitor. Griff looked down at Miranda. She gave him a half-hearted smile, but he must not have bought it.

"Sounds like she needs her diaper changed," he said. "It's my turn for the next two weeks since I just got back from deployment."

"You talked me into it." Miranda waved her arm and watched Griff walk out of the bedroom. She rolled over and hugged his pillow and listened intently. Another one of her greedily hoarded secrets was that she loved listening in when Griff talked to their daughter. He didn't just talk nonsense, nope, he talked about his hopes and dreams for his little girl.

Miranda wiped away a tear. Imagine a father wanting the world for his daughter. A father who adored his daughter.

By the time Griffin came back, she had herself back under control and a smile firmly in place.

"It's a damn good thing today is Saturday," he said as he eased into bed. "We're sure not getting much sleep."

"Well, we are now. Turn out the light."

She watched as he turned off the lamp, but even in the darkness she saw his intent stare.

"What?" she asked.

"I need to hear more."

She was going to protest, but then realized that tonight was the night to share. Maybe not everything. But this. At least this.

THREE YEARS Earlier

"SCARLETT," Miranda cried out. She felt tears threatening again and thought about baseball to force back the wetness.

No wonder the woman hadn't been able to hear her. She was hanging out of one of the broken windows. It almost looked like she had been trying to crawl out of the train.

"Miranda, did I hear you call Scarlett's name?"

"Josiah?" She turned her light toward his voice. He was a few yards away, climbing over wreckage. "Yes, I found her. She's partially covered by this seat, and it looks like she tried to climb out a window."

Tufts of seagrass surrounded Scarlett's torso, and the scent of the ocean wafted inside the railcar. "I can't tell how badly she's injured because her head and shoulders are outside."

"I'll be right there."

Miranda still needed to find the baby. The little girl could be anywhere. Miranda's gut told her she was somewhere near Scarlett. Please say she was right.

She heard a crash, then a scream. She turned her light to see what had made the noise.

"Is everyone all right? What happened?" It was Griff's voice.

"I'm fine." A woman answered. "It was a luggage rack and suitcases that fell. It scared me."

Miranda could hear Jeremy crying, then she heard Susan start singing 'The Wheels on the Bus' to distract him. A hand touched her shoulder and she jumped.

"Whoa there, it's me," Josiah said. "Where's Scarlett?" She could hear the underlying panic in his voice.

She pointed her phone's flashlight at Scarlett's prone figure. She was pretty sure she'd seen her breathing, but she couldn't get to her because of the seat.

Josiah sucked in a deep breath at the sight of his wife, then he lifted the seat as if it weighed nothing and knelt next to her. Ever so slowly, he began to pull her back into the railcar, doing his best to support her head and neck as he did so. Miranda didn't realize she had been holding her breath until she saw Scarlett's eyelids twitch.

The woman's lips moved. Miranda was pretty sure she formed the name, "Josiah."

"I'm here for you, Scarlett Ann. I've got you, Love." His hands gently took inventory of her body. She moaned in pain as he ran his hands lightly over her ribs.

She must have said something, or tried to, because he put his ear to her mouth, and then responded. "I'd never give up hope. You know better than that," he said fervently.

She shook her head and moaned.

"Don't move," he admonished. "At the very least, you have broken ribs." He was still palpitating her sides and abdomen, watching her face intently.

"Down there," Scarlett moved her arm, pointing to the window. She gasped in pain. "Hope."

Miranda finally understood what she was saying. She was talking about the baby.

Hope must be outside the train.

Miranda dove down beside where Scarlett lay.

"Dammit, be careful," Josiah growled at Miranda.

"I am," Miranda assured him. "I need to look out the window." Miranda stuck her head out the bent frame, trying to push out some of the safety glass.

"What are you doing?" Josiah demanded to know. He was clearly agitated.

Miranda kept scanning the area. First right, then left. Finally she spotted a little pink tennis shoe that was attached to a miracle.

"Hope," she called out in a sing song voice, trying to get the little girl's attention without scaring her.

The baby was curled up in the fetal position, her eyes open and glassy, sand covering her little face.

"Hope, please answer me, Sweetie. Your mama is worried about you." The child continued to stare off into nothing.

Screech.

The sound was deafening. The train slid even closer to the cliff and Miranda watched in horror as the outside of the train hovered another inch closer above the fragile body of the child. Two feet of space separated Hope from tons of metal. The train lurched again.

"Oww." Miranda's shoulder was slammed into some of the remaining glass of the window. She felt it tear through her blouse and rip into the flesh of her upper arm.

"Are you okay, Miranda?" Josiah asked.

"I'm fine."

"Get back in here," he ordered.

She ignored him and continued to wriggle out toward the toddler. "Hope, Sweetie, come here and I'll take you to your mommy."

She saw a momentary flicker of recognition at the word Mommy. Miranda held out her arms. She was about sixteen feet away from the girl. She'd have to get out of the train in order to reach her.

Strong hands pulled at Miranda's waist.

"Get your ass back in here." She'd never heard Griff sound so angry. Miranda kicked backwards. Ow!

Was the man solid muscle?

She tried to look backwards, but with the grass and her hair, she couldn't see him. "Griff, let me go."

"No. Get back inside."

Miranda kicked again, hoping to hit something a little more vulnerable, but instead she only managed to cause pain to her injured leg.

"What's wrong, why did you cry out in pain?" Griff demanded to know.

"Hope is out here, dammit. Let me go so I can get her." Griff's grip didn't let up. She looked back at Hope and her heart jumped into her throat. The little girl was looking at her fearfully because she'd yelled. She was beginning to scooch backwards toward the edge of the cliff.

"No, Sweetie, come to me," Miranda said in her most soothing voice. "Remember, I'm Jeremy's friend. I'm going to take you to your mommy."

There was a slight shake of Hope's head. She was hearing Miranda, but she wasn't buying what she was selling, and she moved even farther away.

Miranda wanted to cry.

She wanted to scream.

This time when Griff pulled her inside, she didn't resist. Not that she could have, he was a mass of determined muscle. Nope, the right course of action was to go inside, punch him in the nose, or grab him by the balls, and make him listen.

In less than a second, she was face-to-face with an angry alpha male.

"Miranda, what on God's green earth were you thinking? Look at you. You're bleeding like a stuck pig. My God, Honey, you need help."

He was tearing at a shirt he had in his hands to use a bandage, but his eyes never wavered from hers. She'd been ready to go toe-to-toe with him, when she suddenly recognized the bone-deep fear underneath the anger.

"Didn't you hear me? Hope's out there." She saw that it took a moment for it to register.

"The baby?"

"Yes." She scanned the area and saw that Josiah had Scarlett's shirt open and was binding up her ribcage. She also saw a huge hematoma on her abdomen, it was clear that blood was pooling there. It was not good. She wasn't conscious. That explained why Griff wasn't understanding what was going on. "Hope's about fifteen or twenty feet away from the window of the train," Miranda said as she tried to stand up straight. She failed. Griff put his arms around her, taking her weight.

"Griff," her voice trembled. "Hope's next to the cliff. I was trying to get her to crawl over to me, but then I yelled and she scooched away." Miranda buried her face in his chest. It was all too much.

There's no crying in baseball, Slade. Suck it up.

But before she could push herself away from him, she felt his hand stroke her hair and her heart crumpled for an instant as she soaked in the comfort of his caress.

"You're hurt, Honey. Let me help you sit down, and I'll go get her."

Miranda bit her lip, then swore under her breath.

"What?" Griff asked.

"I don't think she'll come to you. She was scared of me, I'm not sure she'll go to you."

"Honey, I've got this, trust me." He brushed a kiss against her forehead. He lowered her gently to the floor where there was magically a pile of soft clothes for her to sit on, so she wasn't on glass. He set her back against a mangled seat.

"I'll be right back." And then he was out the window.

Miranda couldn't help herself. She pushed up off her little nest and crammed her face into the little bit of space available between Griff's ass and the broken window.

Miranda watched in horror as the little girl threw up her hand and wailed the word, "No!" as soon as she saw Griff. Hope must have scrambled two feet backwards toward the cliff.

"Hope," he whispered, a smile in his voice.

"No!" Hope's little voice was even more shrill the second time. This time, she put out two hands, it was a clear sign she wanted him to stop.

"Okay, Honey. I'll go away. Don't move. Please just stay still." Miranda banged her head against the window frame as Griff carefully worked his way back into the train.

When Griff got back inside, he looked at Miranda, his face a mask of frustrated fear. "Where's her Mom?" he asked.

"Susan has a broken leg. A head wound, too. She can't help." Miranda barely kept the tremor from her voice, but it was tough. Griff gathered her in his arms, and for the second time she allowed herself to be comforted.

"Griff, it has to be me. I need to be the one to go out there and get her," she said as she pushed up to look him in the eye.

Griff hesitated. She put her hand on his chest. "Please help me do this."

"I don't want to," he answered, soft and honest.

"But you will, won't you?" She knew this man.

He nodded.

He turned from her. "Billy," he bellowed. "Bring the leash! Bring it fast. Follow the light circling on the ceiling." He flashed his light at the ceiling.

"Who's Billy?"

"Never mind," he said as he took a peek under the makeshift bandage on her upper arm. She knew that it was still seeping blood. "Dammit, woman, you sure did a number on yourself."

She sucked in a deep breath as he gently touched her wound.

"Griff? Captain?" A young man's voice sounded somewhere nearby. She saw a gangly blond teenager slowly come into view.

"We're here, what's the ETA on your brother?" Josiah asked.

"They see the train. He said to tell you both that they're coordinating with someone named Dex from your team, Griff."

Miranda watched as the young man in a wetsuit and tennis shoes climbed over two seats and thrust what looked like a rope at Griff.

"How's Scarlett?" Miranda asked Josiah.

"She's in and out of consciousness," he said in a tight voice.

It had been a stupid question.

Josiah pulled out his phone and pressed a number. "McAllister? What the fuck is going on?"

Miranda watched as emotions played over the older man's face. Finally, she saw a look of relief. "Yeah, requesting some of the equipment from Camp Pendleton is great. You go to the Admiral if you need to."

Josiah actually grinned at something the man on the other end of the phone was saying. Miranda would bet her bottom dollar that the man said he had already gone to the admiral.

Okay, that was one aspect of the rescue handled, but what about the rest? "Griff, why aren't we swarming with Emergency personnel?" Miranda asked.

"Honey, it might seem like hours, but it hasn't even been a half-hour."

That couldn't be right.

"But, shouldn't they be here by now, even if it has been just a half-hour?" she asked.

"We're not near a road, it's hard for them to make it. But they sent a helicopter, and we heard them pounding on the side of the train."

"And—" Josiah started to say something.

"What?" she demanded. Both men stayed silent. "Tell me, I need to know."

"There's smoke coming from the rail car next to this one, and fire coming from the lead engine," Billy blurted out. "That's the one they'll be working on first."

"Thank you for telling me." She gave the teen a tight smile. "Okay, then we're on our own. Got it. I'm used to that. Now help me get to Hope," she said, looking up at Griff.

This big man who had come to mean so much to her looked down at her, his eyes dark with resolve. "This is how it's going to work. No deviating from the plan, got it, Slade?" When he didn't continue, she reluctantly nodded. "I'm going to tie this leash to your uninjured foot. Then you're going to crawl out there, keeping your body as low to the ground as possible. That will help keep the earth stable. You with me?"

She nodded again.

He turned so that his back was to Billy and Josiah. Then he bent down so that their eyes were just inches apart. "You are not going to let one bad thing happen to you. I want a whole hell of a lot more than just a date. I haven't chased you for nine weeks to let you slip away this easily."

Miranda barked out a laugh, then clapped her hand over her mouth. She felt like shit that she had actually laughed at a time like this.

"This? This is slipping away easy? You need your sense of reality checked, Mr. Porter."

He bent down and brushed a kiss against her lips.

How in the hell could she be laughing and responding to a kiss in the middle of hell?

"You stay safe. Now let me get this secured." He started to bend down to tie the leash on her ankle, when she gripped his wrist.

"It's not long enough."

"It's plenty long enough." He cupped her cheeks and stared deep into her eyes. "I'm going to be hanging out the window holding onto the leash, I'm six foot two, add the length of my arm, and that's plenty of extra length."

"You can't come outside. If she sees you, she'll freak. This is all predicated on you staying out of sight. Just your long-assed arm can be outside. So, I'm telling you, the leash is too short."

"Under no circumstances do you take off the leash, are we clear?"

At least this time she remembered not to bite her lip. "Do you want me to lie to you, Griffin?"

"What?" His voice was a low rumble.

"I'll lie if I have to. Is that what you want?"

"No."

"Good, because I'll do anything to save this girl. Please trust me to do what's smart. Put the leash on me. But know this, if push comes to shove and I need to untie this damn thing in order to save that little girl, I'm going to damn well untie it."

She'd never seen dark eyes shimmer with such heat. "Fine," he ground out. "But *you* know this, I'll come after you." And somehow, she did know it. Here in the middle of all this uncertainty, Miranda was absolutely positive that Griffin Porter would move heaven and earth to reach her if she should need him.

She put her hand on his shoulders and he got down on his knees as he securely fastened the nylon around her ankle. He helped her out the window, after ensuring that all of the glass had been removed. As soon as she got a good look outside, her heart sank. The toddler had moved even farther away from the train.

Miranda crawled just a little, then she propped herself cross-legged on the ground, like she had seen day care teachers do on television. "Sweetie," she crooned. "Can you come here?" The toddler looked at her with a lost and frightened stare. Carefully and slowly, so as not to scare her, she held out her arms in the universal gesture of welcome. "Your mommy's waiting for you. We have milk. Aren't you thirsty?"

Finally she got a small nod.

Success!

"Can you come closer?"

The little girl moved slightly toward her, but then stopped as she slipped in the sand. She held out one chubby little hand.

"Well okay then, Sweetheart, I'll come to you."

Miranda used her elbows to propel herself forward. She was feeling claustrophobic with the side of the train just a mere foot above her head.

Don't think about it, Slade.

Sand was getting inside her blouse, and underneath the top of her skirt. Everything about this was making her skin crawl.

"Milk," Hope said as she continued to hold out her arms and snap her hands open and shut.

"Yes, your mommy has milk waiting for you," Miranda lied easily. She would promise anything to keep the girl happy.

"Wan' Mama."

"Stay right there, and I'll get you and take you to your Mama."

Miranda continued to use her elbows to crawl toward Hope, but then the little girl got anxious and decided to move in Miranda's direction. She plopped down on her hands and knees and tried to go forward, but she was having trouble gaining traction in the sand and sea grass.

"Stop. Hope, wait for me."

The little girl got a stubborn look on her face and grabbed some of the grass and tried to use it to pull herself forward. Yanking the grass pulled it out of the ground and splattered sand and dirt up into her small face.

Hope reared backwards, falling on her bottom, and then she started to cry.

"It's okay, Honey. I'll be right there, and then we'll get you some milk."

Hope continued crying. Then she lifted her closed fists to rub her eyes, and smeared sand into them.

Ah, hell.

The kid was just making everything worse, and her cries turned into sobs.

"It's okay, Baby, I'm almost there." Miranda kept talking, almost in a sing-song voice. "It's going to be just fine. I'll take you to your mom and brother, we'll get you some milk, and get you dressed in warm clothes."

Almost there.

"Then we'll—"

Her body jerked to a stop because of the band around her ankle. She turned and looked behind her.

She saw Griff's expression, fierce and sympathetic. Hope turned her dirt-smeared face to see what she was looking at.

"No!" the baby screeched.

"Griff, get back in the train, you're scaring Hope."

Miranda watched as Hope rolled onto her side, trying to get away from her and Griff.

Enough of this shit.

She reached behind her, losing precious seconds tugging and unknotting the fucking nylon rope. When she turned, Hope was only a foot away from the cliff's edge. Miranda lunged.

"Gotchya."

"No! No! No!"

"I hate the terrible twos." Miranda laughed and cried at the same time as she held the warm little body close to her.

"Dammit, Miranda, you get your ass back here."

"No!" Hope howled the word again.

"You're going to have to learn a new word." Miranda told the child as she turned back toward the train. She spat out some of the sand that had gotten into her mouth, and Hope continued to struggle and say, 'No'.

With her arms full of wiggling child, her feet encased in nylons, and her leg throbbing like a son-of-a-bitch, Miranda was having a hell of time gaining purchase in the sand to get back toward the train.

"Griff," she called out just as the rail car groaned again.

Miranda watched in horrified fascination as the steel behemoth started to lower even more. Would it roll completely on its side, closing off their ability to get back in through the window?

"Griff, come grab Hope," she begged.

Somehow, someway, he was already beside her at the cliff's edge, taking the baby out of her arms.

"Can you follow me?" he asked as he started moving.

"Yes," she assured him. "Just hurry."

As he got Hope to the relative safety of the train's interior, Miranda pushed out with her feet, pushing at the crumbling sand and dirt to follow them. Why was it crumbling? What the hell? She felt the earth begin to give beneath her knees.

Oh God, she was going to go over the side of the cliff!

She made a desperate grab for some sea grass.

MIRANDA STOPPED TALKING and looked up at Griff.

"Do you remember falling?" he asked.

Miranda shook her head.

He had been holding her, swirling designs on her skin with his thumb. But as soon as she talked about taking the leash off her ankle, he'd been frozen. It had taken everything she had to continue talking. She rushed through the last little bit of the story. Well, at least Griff didn't have to ask if she was done. Her ending was kind of clear.

"So you don't remember anything but clutching at sea grass?" he asked.

Apparently it wasn't clear.

"No. The doctors were surprised I remembered as much as I did. They said in a lot of cases like mine that the hours before and after the event would be wiped out of the patient's memory banks."

"Hmmm."

What did that mean?

"Griff?"

"I'm hungry." He pushed up from the bed. "I'm going to make some eggs. Do you want some?"

"It's three-thirty in the morning."

"I was just on the other side of the world four days ago, my hours are all screwed up. It feels like time to eat."

He wasn't looking at her, and his jaw was so tight it looked like it might shatter. Miranda turned on the light and scrambled to the dresser. She pulled on a pair of pajama bottoms and a sweatshirt, then followed her husband into the kitchen.

She watched as he pulled food out of the refrigerator. She'd bet her next paycheck that if Livvie weren't around, he'd be banging the frying pan onto the stove.

"Are you mad?" she asked tentatively.

He carefully cracked the eggs into a mixing bowl. "How would you like your eggs cooked?" he asked politely.

"I'm not hungry. Answer my question. Are you mad at me?"

He looked sideways at her. "I can't be, now can I? That'd just make me an irrational asshole."

Noting that he'd scrambled enough for the two of them and poured them into the pan, she sighed and put bread into the toaster.

She came up behind him, wrapped her arms around his waist and pressed her cheek against his back. "I love you, even if you *are* irrational. Tonight's our night for truth-telling. The good, the bad and the ugly."

She felt him tense.

He kept stirring the eggs. "If I tell you how fucking mad I was at you for taking off that leash, even though you ended up saving Hope, what then? I was scared out of my head. But the guys and I make those kinds of decisions every day. I wouldn't bat an eyelash if Dalton had made that call, fuck, I'd have applauded. But you?"

She kissed his spine.

"Keep talking," she coaxed.

He turned off the gas and moved the pan off the burner. He turned around so he could look down at her.

"Most days." He winced. "Scratch that. For almost three years, I've looked at that little girl and she brightens my life. But today, my heart twisted. For a few seconds, I remembered what it was like when you handed me her warm body and I watched you grapple not to fall."

"Did you resent her, or were mad at me for making the choice to save her?"

She watched him struggle to answer.

"I'm not going to judge you, Griff. Tonight is for

truth. You've been holding this in for three long years, Honey. Just tell me."

"God," he bit out. "I was mad at God. Fury raced through me at that instant. I was mad at him for punishing my dad, for killing those people, for damn near killing this baby in my arms. And the worst was for forcing you to make the only choice you possibly could."

He dropped his forehead down onto hers. He continued, his voice hoarse. "I wanted to scream. But I had to just do the job. I'd never been so out of control in my life, then I was mad at me. I almost lost it at the most crucial time of my life."

His anguish shone through. "How can I have such an ugly truth and be any type of father to our daughter?"

Miranda was stunned. When they'd started talking this through tonight, she'd been sure she'd find he was holding deep-seated anger at her. She should have known better. She leaned forward to lay a kiss on his heart, but he stopped her.

"No. Don't try pawning me off with some bullshit comfort. Answer the question."

"I'm not comforting you. I'm thanking you. I'm thanking you for not screaming. For not losing it. For not resenting Hope. For understanding why I did what I did and loving me. This isn't comfort, this is love."

She looked up at him and his eyes gleamed. This time he didn't push her away when she laid a kiss over his heart.

7

"I don't deserve you." He felt like a weight that he hadn't even known had been perched on his shoulder was suddenly gone. He hooked his arm around her shoulders. "Let's go to bed.

"Now I'm hungry. How about pancakes?" Miranda suggested.

Oh, he was fucked. If she was buttering him up with pancakes, then she wanted something, and he knew what it was.

"Seriously, I'm tired." He faked a yawn.

"I want pancakes," she said as she reached in the pantry for the syrup and the pancake mix.

"You want to talk some more," he sighed.

"Correction, I want you to talk some more. I spilled my guts, but you've never really told me what it was like when you climbed down the cliff."

He thrust his hand through his hair. "Please, I'm begging you, let's go to bed." He kept a smile in his voice. Maybe charm would work. She watched as she continued to mix the batter.

"I'm making pancakes. I'm making enough for both of us, you can stay up and eat some with me, or you can go to bed. Your choice."

God, she was a stubborn wench!

"I already told you I was mad at God. What more do you want from me?"

She set down the whisk and leaned her elbows against the counter and looked at him. She bit her lip. "I remember bits and pieces of what you told me when I was in the hospital, but that's all. It's just bits and pieces. I guess I unconsciously knew this was a tough subject for you, so I didn't ask more. I didn't ask the tough stuff But now that we're at it, I just want to know. Is that so wrong?"

"You didn't remember what we talked about in the hospital?"

She shook her head.

How come he hadn't realized that?

"I want five pancakes," he said.

She gave him a relieved grin and turned back to the batter.

Three Years Earlier

HOLDING ONTO HOPE, Griff saw Miranda's desperate attempt to stop her fall. Her pale hand clutching blanched green stalks of sea grass was the last thing he saw before she toppled over the side of the cliff.

He knew it was at least a hundred foot drop, but it was graded, so it was possible she'd landed on some resting spot before hitting the beach below. He had to get to her.

"Billy, take Hope." He tried to thrust the baby at the young man, but now she was hanging on for dear life.

"No!" Hope shouted with a tearful scream as he pried her hands from around his neck to give her to Billy.

The train was making a deafening sound as it tipped even more. Griff heard the tortured yell 'No' rip out of his throat right along with the child's cries. He looked down at the window at his feet. The space between the window frame and the sand was now miniscule. There was no way he could possibly squeeze through.

"Billy, I need you to find this girl's mom. She should be that way." Griff pointed the opposite way from where Billy had come.

"Okay." He took the screaming baby. "Here's my phone. Mason wanted to talk to you," he told Griff above the baby's cries. He started to rock her and stroke her back. "Mason's going to call when he and Drake get onto the top of the rail car." Billy shook his head. "I mean, the side of it."

"I know what you meant," Griff assured him. "But how will he know which one we're in?"

"I told my buddy Jaden to stay up top and direct traffic."

The rocking seemed to help. Hope's crying was turning into snuffles.

"What's the mom's name?" Billy asked.

"Susan," Josiah and Griff answered simultaneously.

"Got it."

"Hold on, Billy. Take my cell phone." Griff handed his over. "You can use it for light." He rattled off his passcode. "Call if you need us."

"Hand that over," Josiah demanded. "I'll plug my number in."

While they waited, Griff tried to think through how in the hell he was going to get to Miranda. When Josiah was done, Billy took the phone.

"You ready for an adventure?" Billy said soothingly to the child. She hiccupped and looked up at him in fascination. The young man flashed the light and started to pick his way toward the back.

"What happened?" Josiah asked as soon as Billy was out of earshot.

Griff took a look at Scarlett, who was out cold, but still taking in air. That was good. He turned back to look at his captain.

"As soon as she got a hold of Hope, I got my ass out there. She shoved the baby at me and I bolted for the train." Griff swallowed, replaying the moment in his mind. "I thought she was behind me. I didn't realize she would have any trouble following. It's my fault. By the time I got inside the train with Hope, I turned around and saw that Miranda was damn near where I'd left her. Then." Griff stopped and gulped. "Then the ground beneath her gave way. She went over the side." He said steadily.

Josiah clasped Griff's shoulder. "It's not your fault. You did the right thing, it was the mission. It was what Miranda wanted. Now we focus on the second part. Remember, the cliff wasn't a straight drop," Josiah said as he cradled his wife in his arms.

Griff wanted Miranda in *his* arms.

"I'm going out to get her. I'll tell the men where you are," Griff told Josiah.

"Let me give you Billy's phone. That way when Mason calls, you can take it." Griff thrust the phone to the older man.

Josiah shook his head. "I have him on speed dial, no need."

Griff should have known. He watched as Josiah stroked back a lock of Scarlett's hair, then looked back up at him. "Now, go get your woman." With that, he bent his head back down next to Scarlett's and whispered something in her ear. Griff sent up a silent prayer for both women.

FOR SOME REASON, Griff had thought it would be better once he got outside of the rail car. He was wrong. Instead, it was another kind of hell. The lead car was the power car and it was on fire. The next one was the closest to him, the business rail car, before there had just a wisp of smoke floating above it, now it was shrouded in black furls of smoke. He looked at the landscape surrounding them and realized there wasn't a chance in fucking hell that fire trucks could reach them. No wonder there were military Humvees driving up along with various civilian trucks.

He so wanted to walk to the other side of the top of the car, near the cliff, to see if he could spy Miranda, but he was concerned that his weight could shift the precarious position of the train.

"Griff?"

He turned and saw a huge man peering up at him. He vaguely recognized him as the second-in-command of the Midnight Delta SEAL team, Drake Avery.

"We're coming up," the man shouted. He was talking about himself and two other men beside him. One of them had to be his lieutenant, Mason Gault, Billy's brother.

"Don't come up. We have a problem. I'm coming down."

Griff ran to the end of the car and found the handholds necessary to climb down. On his way, he met three men who were working to uncouple the downed car from the dining car. They were struggling with the equipment. Nothing seemed to be going right. Drake met him when he reached the ground.

"This is Mason, my lieutenant," Drake introduced quickly. "The other guy is our communications/tech guru, Clint Archer. Whatchya got?" Drake asked.

"A woman who means a hell of a lot to me fell down the side of the cliff when she rescued a baby," he said as he pointed between the two rail cars. Nothing more needed to be said, Griff could see that they were immediately in mission mode.

"I brought some supplies with me." Drake indicated the duffel at his feet. "I've got other shit that we might need, in my truck." Drake took off at a dead run.

"The Humvees are equipped with cable. They're planning on securing the train so it doesn't slip any more than it has. We can commandeer some of that," Mason said.

Griff looked over and saw emergency crews and Marines hooking up the cable to the bottom of the downed rail car. He also saw men working to open the entry door so that people could be evacuated. Shit, he recognized Hunter and Dalton. Hunter was a new guy on his team. He was using an exothermic torch.

"How many people are in that car? How's Billy?" Mason asked.

"Billy's been a big help," Griff answered. "He's got a great head on his shoulders. As for how many people are on the car, I don't know. If I had to hazard a guess, I'd say about forty-five on the top floor, and I saw at least eight bodies. I have no idea how many on the first floor."

Drake came back with his hands full and a skein of rope hanging from his right shoulder.

"An EMT is getting in touch with one of the choppers," Clint Archer said as he looked up from his smart phone. "When you find your woman, they'll send down a basket."

"Where are we going?" Drake asked.

Griff led them past the back of the rail car. "Billy

and his friends climbed up the cliff at one point. They shouldn't have. It was too fucking dangerous," Griff said as he pointed around the side of the train.

"They're teenagers," was Mason's succinct explanation.

The sun was behind them as they looked out into the water. Griff's every instinct was screaming at him to run to the side of the cliff, but he knew it was foolish. They needed to go slow and make sure that the ground beneath them was firm. The weight of the train had destabilized the cliff.

"Where did she go over?" Drake asked.

"Near the middle of the car. You can see where the landslide occurred," he said pointing to where there was a significant drop off.

"Got it," Mason said.

"Drake was already unwrapping the rope. "We can tie it off on the train."

"It's too unstable," Griff protested.

"Nope, by the time we have our first knot tied, the Marines will have enough cables on it to ensure the fucker isn't going anyplace," Clint said. He was listening to his phone.

"Be sure," Griff commanded.

Clint listened some more, then grinned and gave a thumbs up.

"We're good to go. The big issue now is to evacuate the wounded."

Drake was already tying the rope, and Griff was grabbing the other end to tie around his waist.

"Nope," Mason said. "Me first. I surf this beach all

the damn time. I've also climbed up this damn cliff a time or two." Griff gave him a long look, then handed him the end of the rope.

Mason rappelled over the side of the cliff, and Griff was a hairsbreadth behind him. He looked over his shoulder, and didn't see Miranda anywhere on the sand and rocks below them. His entire body shuddered in relief.

Mason was already picking his way over to the left, where Miranda had fallen. There was some slope there, so it was possible she could have grabbed hold of a rock or some tufts grass.

Please God, say that she had.

Drake came over the cliff next, and Griff saw that Clint was topside making himself available to direct traffic. Each of them took a twenty-foot section of the cliff, attempting to make sure that they didn't miss anything. They went slowly, scanning every nook and cranny

"I see her," Mason shouted out.

"Where?" Griff demanded.

"Directly beneath Drake. She's landed against a rock. She's hidden by the seagrass, but you can see a bit of pink."

Now that Mason pointed her out, he could see a nylon-clad leg. Drake had his phone out, Griff saw that he was taking a picture, probably sending it up to Clint. Then Griff saw that his phone was up to his ear.

"The chopper will be here within ten minutes with a rescue basket." Drake called out. "They're coming back from the hospital at Palomar. Let's get your lady ready for transport." He shoved his phone back into his cargo pants.

God love Drake Avery, he just took it at face value that Miranda was alive. They made their way down to her, careful not to knock any debris loose that might land on her. Mason reached her first, but Griff was there within seconds.

"She's alive," Mason grinned at him, his fingers on the pulse of her neck.

"Miranda, can you hear me?" Griff asked urgently.

He ran his hands gently over her body for signs of injury. How could her pearls be resting perfectly around her neck? It seemed wrong.

Her wrist was obviously broken, and there was blood at the back of her head. Carefully, Griff guided his fingers around her head, probing softly, until he got to the back of her skull. He almost cried in relief when he felt the back of her skull and found that it wasn't crushed, there just seemed to be a cut and swelling.

Thank you, God.

Did he see and eyelash flicker?

"Miranda. Oh Baby, you were supposed to take better care of yourself." His voice broke. "Honey, I'm here for you. Now, I did my part, you do your part and stay with me, okay? You promised." He brushed a kiss against her cheek. "You promised, Miranda." His voice broke.

Griff heard the *whomp whomp* of the helicopter. Drake was kneeling against the side of the cliff and waving. Griff saw someone stick their hand out of the chopper and wave back. Soon, the helicopter lowered a rescue stretcher. Mason and he steadied it.

Griff wanted to be the one who placed Miranda in the basket, but ultimately it was Mason who did it with Griff's help. They ever so gently placed Miranda into the pallet and strapped her in. Griff tugged on the rope and gave the team in the helicopter a thumbs-up and they raised her up.

He scrambled up the cliff, determined to be at the hospital as soon as humanly possible.

8

THREE YEARS EARLIER

"MOM'S AWAKE."

Griff jerked at the feel of his Nick Hales's big hand on his shoulder. Before he acknowledged his friend's words, he soaked in Miranda's still form in the hospital bed. He couldn't believe how much worse she looked after surgery. Her face was swollen, and her eyes looked like she had been in a bar fight. Seeing the rise and fall of her breathing calmed him down.

He stroked her lower left arm, which was all that was available to him to touch and hold. Her hand had a clip to monitor her pulse clamped to it, and there were so many IV's and wires attached everywhere else, she seemed like some kind of science experiment. Finally he turned to glance over his shoulder at Josiah Hale's son.

"How's your mom doing?" Griff asked. As much as

he worried for Miranda, he knew that Scarlett had been in critical condition.

"Good. They had to take out her spleen. Dad said that without Liam organizing your team on-site, she wouldn't have made it."

Nick paused and looked at Miranda. "How's Miranda doing?" he asked solemnly.

"They say the surgery went well. Now is the time for waiting."

"And you hate waiting."

Griff nodded.

Both men's eyes turned to the door before it even opened. Griff had recognized the sound of Shelly's footsteps prior to her coming inside the room.

She nodded a smile at Nick, then turned to Griff.

"Griff, you heard what the doctors said, Miranda's not going to wake up for a couple of days. Why don't you go home and get some rest?"

He looked up into the eyes of the kind nurse. She'd been on duty since Miranda had been brought into ICU. Griff knew that she was newly-married, and was planning on having a dozen children.

"I just can't stand the idea of her waking up without a friendly face around."

"Are you saying my face isn't friendly?" Shelly asked, her hands on her hips. Griff gave a wan smile.

"You're beautiful, Shel," but his eyes darted back to Miranda. He couldn't help it. He needed to keep her in his sights. "Can she hear me?" he asked.

"Ah Honey, I believe she can."

Griffin stood up and bent over the bed. He brushed

a kiss against her swollen cheek and whispered in her ear. "You're the most beautiful woman I've ever met, Miranda Slade. I can't wait to see your blue eyes again."

"Griff, you really need to get out of here and get some rest," Shelly said gently.

"I can't."

"Yes you can," Nick inserted. "I hate to tell you this, but you're smelling kind of ripe. Now, unless you're thinking that some kind of body odor aromatherapy is going to bring her around, do the girl a favor and shower before she wakes up."

"But she doesn't have anyone else. All of her friends are back East or on some film location, and her parents are dead."

"We've got you covered," a deep voice said. This time Griff was taken by surprise as he turned to the opened hospital room door. He spun around to see his former teammate, Jack Preston, and his fiancée, Beth Hidalgo standing beside him.

Griff swallowed twice, then he went over and thrust out his hand. Jack pulled him in for a hug instead.

"How'd you know to be here?" Griff asked Jack. He had no memory of him being at the crash site.

"There can only be two visitors at one time in the ICU," Shelly said.

"Griff, Nick and I are just leaving," Jack said. "Beth, come with us into the hallway for a moment, so we can fill Griff in on our plan."

"Did Gray tell you?" Griff asked, referring to his lieutenant of the Black Dawn SEAL team.

"Hell, Man, everybody told me. You can't take a turn

around anywhere in Coronado without hearing about your woman, the Amtrak heroine."

"Gray also explained she doesn't have any family, and you were watching over her. We want to help you." Beth's smile was sweet.

"So, here's the deal," Jack continued. "Captain Hale filled Gray in, he wanted to be here first, but realized that he needed to start sending those of us with significant others. I can't think of anyone better than my Beth to be here for your Miranda," Jack said with pride and love.

"But you don't know her," Griff protested as he looked at the attractive Hispanic woman.

"I've met you a few times." Beth's voice was as gentle as the hand she laid on his arm. "You're like a brother to Jack. You served together for years before he left Black Dawn to serve with Midnight Delta. I know what it's like to rely on the kindness of strangers, and I want to pay that kindness back to Miranda."

"Griff, you're no good to her right now, you need to get some sleep," Nick admonished.

Griff dug his truck keys out of his jeans pocket. "I'll—"

He looked at both Nick and Jack's raised eyebrows.

Ah hell, his truck was back up in L.A. near the train station.

Nick laughed. "You are so out of it. Were you thinking your truck was here at the hospital?"

Griff nodded.

"Give me the key to your truck. It's up near your folk's place at the train station, right?" Nick asked.

Griff hesitated, looking over at Beth. "Jack programmed your number into my phone, Griffin. I'll call you immediately if something changes. I promise," she said as she held up her cell phone.

"Thank you." He watched as she opened the door to Miranda's room and heard Shelly greet her.

"I'm going back to Mom's room," Nick said. He held out his hand. Griff took his house key off the ring and pocketed it, then gave over the keys to his truck. Nick turned to go down the hall, then he paused mid-step and turned around. "Brother?" He looked directly into Griff's eyes.

"Yeah?"

"I'll never fucking forget what you did for my mother. Never." Nick did a one-eighty and swiftly continued down the hall.

Griff let out a deep breath, then tilted his chin to Jack. "Let's go."

Jack nodded, and they headed to the elevator. Soon they were out in the warm night air. When they got to Jack's SUV, the man immediately rolled down the windows. Griff grimaced. Nick was right, he did stink.

The last thing Griff remembered doing was buckling his seat belt, then Jack was nudging him. "Home sweet home."

Looking up, he gave a tired smile. "Want to come inside?" he asked Jack.

"That was kind of the plan," Jack grinned. "I'm your chauffer back to the hospital, remember?"

Shit, he was out of it.

The two of them trudged up the couple of stairs to

the front door and Griff let them in. He offered Jack something to drink.

"Why don't I just help myself to some water while you go get cleaned up?" Jack suggested.

Griff nodded, and headed down the hall to his bedroom. "I'll be out in a few." He damn near fell into the shower.

God, it felt good.

He leaned his head against the shower wall and pictured Miranda in the hospital bed and replayed what the doctor had said. She was going to need her family when she first left the hospital, and she'd need round-the-clock care for almost a month.

When Griff had explained that Miranda didn't have a family, the medical team immediately started talking about in-patient convalescent care, and his had blood run cold. It went against everything he believed in, it sure as hell wasn't where his Miranda belonged. She needed to be with people who cared. She needed to be with him.

How in the hell was he going to convince her? Rolling a bolder uphill would be easier.

His mouth twitched up in a tired grin. After seeing her bloodied and then in a coma, the idea of Miranda spitting fire at him was welcome.

While drying off, he surveyed his bathroom with a critical eye. He did the same thing with his bedroom as he got dressed. Walking out to the living room he took note of the hallway and determined that even though it was narrow, it should be able to accommodate a walker, but a wheelchair would be touch and go.

"Do you want a sandwich?" he asked Jack as he opened his fridge.

"I already placed a to-go order for steak sandwiches, fish tacos and carnitas tacos with all the sides at the Snack Shack. We're picking them up on the way back to the hospital." Griff's stomach growled at the thought as he grabbed a bottle of fruit juice and shut the refrigerator.

Jack leaned against the kitchen island and gave Griff a hard look. "So tell me about Miranda."

"I waited too fucking long."

"What do you mean?" Jack asked.

"I should have asked her out the first time I saw her. I knew she was special. I've been jonesing for her for almost two damn months. I've been taking public transportation instead of driving my perfectly fine truck, just so I could see her. Mom thought it was cute. Dad thought it was funnier than hell."

"You mean you, Griffin Porter, gave up a chance to sing along with the country radio station?"

"I know, right?" Griff agreed. "Anyway, my truck was in the shop the first time I took the train. That was when I met her. It was fixed the next week, but there wasn't a chance in hell I was going to miss an opportunity to see her again."

"Why didn't you just ask her out?" Jack took a sip of water. It was obvious he was really curious.

"Because Dad's been so sick. The chemo was really kicking his ass, and I've been a morose piece of shit to be around. Mom's called me almost every night of the week when I wasn't up there on the weekends. Dating just wasn't in the cards. But this weekend? This weekend Dad lit up, and I knew it was my chance."

"What were you thinking so hard about just now when you were coming out of the bedroom?"

"You kind of suck, you know that?" Griff asked his friend as he finished his juice and threw the bottle in his recycle bin and slouched into the corner of the kitchen counters.

"That's what happens when you spend three years together on a SEAL team. You end up being able to read each other a little too well."

Griff wished that Jack hadn't switched to Mason's team. It hadn't been the same on Black Dawn without him.

"So, what were you thinking?" Jack prompted again.

"I was wondering whether or not I could get this place in working order so that Miranda could recuperate here."

"Hmmm." Jack took a sip out of his glass.

Griff really appreciated that he kept his own counsel. The man didn't jump right in with why he shouldn't take such a big step. Jack had been the most laidback and thoughtful of all the team members. He was even more relaxed than Hunter Diaz, but that was probably because he was a few years older.

"Out with it," Griff said.

"Are you sure you want questions? Seems to me, you've made up your mind."

"I have, but I like the idea that you might be looking at some angles I haven't covered."

"Reasonable," Jack nodded. "You know she doesn't

have any family. What about other good friends? Wouldn't they take her in?"

"I don't think so. Not a single one of them has come to visit. Sure, they've sent flowers. They've called, but they've had a million and one excuses why they couldn't be here. When we were talking, she said they were all workaholics like her, and she didn't think they would even be able to take a week off to meet up with her for a vacation. I think it's up to me."

"That's an interesting turn of phrase, 'It's up to me.'" Jack straightened away from the kitchen island. "Griff, you're making it sound like it's your responsibility. It's not. You really don't know the woman. You're not in love with her. You haven't even been out on a date with her, have you?"

Griff took his time before answering. "That's the thing Jack, I *do* know her. God, by that second train ride I knew she was someone special. As Dex would say, she's wicked smart and she makes me laugh. I think about her all the time."

Jack nodded for him to continue.

"I know this is going to sound strange, but I got to watch her do her job on the train and she's super-competent. It was a huge turn-on."

"Did she wear a business suit?" Jack asked with a grin. "You've always been a sucker for a woman in a pencil skirt."

"Hell, she sometimes even wore pearls."

Jack laughed. "Yeah, you were doomed. What else?"

"The wreck cinched it for me. I love her. I'm *in* love with her. When I saw her go after Hope…"

"Hope? That's the baby, right?"

"Yep. Miranda waded in without a thought to her own safety to save that little girl. She got in my face and demanded that she be the one to climb out that train window and pluck the kid off the cliff. When I demanded she not take any risks, she shouted me down. She said she'd lie to me if she had to, but don't make her, because she was going to do what the situation required. Fuck, Jack. Need I say more?"

"Let me guess, she took the right risk, and saved the kid."

"Yep, and ended up in that hospital bed because of it. She's a crazy woman, and she's mine to take care of."

"What makes you think she would ever, in a million years, agree to this?"

"I'm not sure she has a choice."

"You mean it's convalescent hospital or you?" Jack asked.

Griff stood up straight and walked around the bar to face the window in the dining room. He could still see Jack. "I can't believe you would think I would throw down on her like that. I would move heaven and earth to make sure she has the best recovery possible, *outside* of a convalescent or rehab facility."

"I call bullshit. You intend to glue her ass beside you."

Griff rubbed a frustrated hand through his short hair. "What's wrong with that? She needs care. I can offer that. Ergo, she needs to stay with me."

"Ah, fuck, you just said 'ergo'. You've lost the argument before it even starts."

"All right, Brainiac, what would you suggest?"

Jack put his empty glass of water in the sink and joined Griff in the dining room. "Are you doing this because you need to fill the void left now that your daddy's getting well?"

Talk about a question coming out of left field. He glared at Jack, then he really took the time to think it through.

"I hated it when Dad was sick. Hated it with a passion. I hated that he felt like shit. He was so weak, and he felt impotent. I wanted to fix it for him. But the fact that he needed help and I could provide it...? To the man who made me who I am today? Yeah, that was a bit of a rush. But that was a miniscule amount of what was behind me doing it. Because I would have given my left nut for him not to have had to go through cancer."

Griff could see Jack's shoulders release some tension.

"This is a whole different ballgame with Miranda. We don't know what to expect when she wakes up. She has a traumatic brain injury. To tell you the truth, depending on the level of care she needs..." Griff's voice trailed off.

"Don't think that way," Jack's hand clamped down on Griff's shoulder.

Griff shook off his melancholy thoughts. "Let's go get the food. The doctors said that there was no damage to her brain. They just had to repair a couple of blood vessels, they really think that there's no reason not to expect a full recovery."

"There you go," Jack said easily as they headed to the front door. "Focus on that."

"I'm going to." Griff said as he locked the door behind him.

They got into the SUV and decided to change the subject. "So when are you and Beth going to tie the knot?"

"You really have been out of it."

"That goes without saying, but humor me, why are you saying it?"

"You should have checked your mail, there should be a wedding invitation in it." Jack pulled into the restaurant's parking lot. "Stay here, I'll be right back."

"I'm paying," Griff said, as he got out his wallet.

"I'm rich," Jack said with a self-deprecating grin. "Put your money away." He slammed the door shut.

Griff pulled out his phone and texted Dex Evans and found out the details of Jack and Beth's upcoming wedding.

"You're thinking pretty hard again," Jack said as he put four bags of food in the backseat.

"Hell, you're getting married in two months in San Antonio."

"Yep." Jack pulled onto the freeway. "Mom's chartered a plane for folks."

"What? Isn't that excessive?"

"That's my mom. She wanted to make sure everyone would be able to make it to the wedding. She remembers when we didn't have two dimes to rub together. It was important to her that everybody who's important to me here in California would be able to make it." Jack had an indulgent look on his face. "So what does your Miranda do for a living?"

"She's a hotshot consultant. She does project management, making sure everybody works to the terms of the agreed upon contract."

"And you think you'll be able to convince her to just move in with you? Again, I say, good luck with that," Jack laughed.

He took the freeway exit to the hospital and Griff considered his friend's point. He was right, he was going to have to be very careful on how he presented his solution to Miranda. He didn't want to have a battle on his hands. However, he was extremely good at battles.

"Are you going into sniper mode?" Jack asked.

"What do you mean?"

"I've seen you wait out the enemy for thirty-two hours. You can be a patient son-of-a-bitch when you get a target in your sites."

"In that case, I guess I am. But I'm using my powers for good."

They were soon at the hospital. When they got to the waiting room, they found Mason and his wife, Sophia, with her little brother Billy Anderson. Most of his Black Dawn team members were there too, along with Drake Avery.

Billy rushed up to Griff, clearly distraught. "They said Miranda is in a coma. Mason said you would know the most. How is she doing? How did the surgery go? When is she going to wake up?"

Griff put both of his hands on the young man's shoulders.

"Breathe, Billy. The surgeon said the operation went perfectly. They were able to alleviate a lot of the swelling and stop some of the bleeding that was happening. As the swelling goes down, she should wake up in a few days."

"Days?" The kid was clearly choked up. He was emoting what Griff was feeling.

"Her brain just needs time to rest and heal. We got her here in time, they don't think there was any brain damage."

"Griff, let us know what we can do to help," Mason said.

"You can tell us where a vending machine is, I didn't get drinks," Jack said holding up the sacks of food.

"Billy's all over that," Sophia said with a smile. She handed her purse to Billy. "You know where the coins are."

"I need to get back in there with Miranda," Griff said, eyeing the hallway.

"No, first you're going to eat." Gray Tyler, his lieutenant said firmly as he stood next to him. At that moment. he realized he was boxed in by him and Jack.

Fuck.

Then his stomach growled.

"Why don't you come sit next to me?" Sophia suggested. She was unpacking the food and laying it out on the table in front of her. He reluctantly sat down, and Gray sat down on his other side. Sophia handed

Griff a steak sandwich, and all reluctance flew out the window as he started eating with gusto.

Most of the men ate standing up. He turned to Gray after he had finished his sandwich. "Have you heard from Josiah? How is Scarlett doing? Did anything change while I was gone?"

"Damn, I forgot for a second that you're family friends with the Captain," Gray said ruefully. "Mrs. Hale is already trying to get out of bed so she can come see Miranda. There were more flowers delivered to Miranda's room. It's getting out of hand. Beth made sure to keep the ones from the Hollister's."

"Who?"

"The baby Miranda rescued? Her name is Hope Hollister. Her dad died in Afghanistan. It was one of her grandparents who arranged for the flowers to be sent. Apparently, her mother is still recuperating after spending a night in the hospital."

"I couldn't believe all the flowers from strangers that were showing up," Griff said. "Fucking-A, Miranda made the national news."

"You don't sound happy about it," Dex said as he sauntered up to grab another fish taco.

"I'm not. I mean, it's great that people are recognizing her heroism, but I don't want her recovery impeded. She's going to need peace and quiet, not a feeding frenzy of reporters."

"But you have a plan, don't you?" Dex said before he took a bite.

"Damn right I do."

MIRANDA'S LAUGH jolted Griff out of his flashback. It took just a moment to realize he was in the present, and that she was not in a hospital bed, but actually sitting across from him at their dining room table, a baby monitor sitting on the table between them.

"Why the laughter?" he asked his beautiful wife.

Miranda lifted her head. She'd had it propped on her palm while her elbow rested on the table. "I'll tell you why the laughter. I don't think I've ever realized that you were actually kind of sneaky. Single minded, determined and a bulldozer, sure. But manipulative? I thought that was more my style."

"What are you talking about?" He didn't know whether to be proud or offended.

"You had been planning your method of attack from the moment I was in the hospital. You were thinking through all of the angles. That is totally a Miranda Slade move."

He leaned over and kissed her. Then he picked up their dishes and dumped them into the sink. It was too late to even think about loading the dishwasher. "Come on, it's time for bed. Livvie's going to be up in two hours. We're going to have to take naps in shifts."

"I'd prefer to take at least one nap together," Miranda said softly as she scooped up the baby monitor.

"That's what I love about Saturdays."

9

MIRANDA GOT TO WORK EARLY ON MONDAY MORNING. Since Griff's team had had a long deployment, he'd taken some of his leave this week so he could take care of Livvie and she could get caught up at work. She shot off two e-mails and stared at the massive size of her inbox stuffed with e-mails that had come in over the weekend. She couldn't concentrate. When she realized she was biting at her thumbnail she damn near threw her hands up in disgust. She needed to get her shit together.

She sat back in her chair and looked at the five pictures on her desk. Susan had put them there. One was of the entire Porter clan, with her, Livvie and Griff in the middle. She was so lucky to be part of this family.

Next was a candid shot that Beth Preston took of Griff leaning over her hospital bed soon after she had woken up. He looked like he hadn't slept in days, but the smile on his face was breathtaking. Just for this picture alone, Beth would always hold a special place in her heart. She turned to the next picture. This was one of her and Griff again, only she had a pissed-off look on her face. Griff said it was her stubborn look and he had a dog-eared copy in his wallet.

It was during these few days that Griff managed to convince her to recuperate at his home. To this day, she had no earthly idea how he could have managed that. She vaguely remembered an argument, but it was so fuzzy, like a dream.

The third picture showed her with her work computer on her lap, and Griff holding her phone over her head with her trying to grab it back from him. Nope, no memory of that.

Yeah, she had been suffering from a severe case of 'like' on the train. Oh hell, who was she kidding, she had a hell of a crush on the big goofy, sexy SEAL. But moving in with him when she was vulnerable as hell? That should have been the last thing she would have ever agreed to, that was *not* her. Not, not, not.

Miranda felt a gooey smile covering her face. If it had been a little bit of brain damage that had caused her to agree, she thanked God for it, because it had been the best decision of her life.

There was a knock on her door and Miranda set down the picture, finally in the mood to get shit done.

"Come in," Miranda called out.

"I brought you some coffee," Susan said as she plunked a Starbuck's cup on her desk. Miranda knew it would be hot and black, just the way she liked it.

"How'd you know I'd be in early?"

Susan rolled her eyes. "You're always in early after Griff's been on deployment. He likes to stay home for a few days and play Mr. Mom."

Miranda took a sip of the black gold and smiled at her assistant. "You are a wonder."

"I know," Susan said impishly as she pulled up a chair. "So what's on today's agenda? Did anything new hit your inbox this weekend?"

"I still have to check," Miranda admitted. "We're going to have to get the lead out. My report that they're going to reference for the meeting with the Joint Chief's is needed in six weeks. We're down to the wire, and I've got a bad feeling. The assholes are being cagey."

Susan's eyes got wide. "Don't tell me that after the international publicity Lartronics received on this project, that they're going to screw it up," she breathed. "Are they giving you a hard time?"

"I don't care about them giving me a hard time, it's the three generals who have my attention. We can't afford to have anything go wrong."

"Wait a minute Miranda, it isn't going to reflect badly on TAID if Lartronics screws-up on delivering this," Susan protested. "Our job was to test everything and give the Pentagon an unbiased assessment of the viability, before they went into production. If you give a green light, or put a stop on it, either way, we're fine. Unless we're trying to get work with Lartronics after this project, is that it?"

"I wish it were that simple. If Lartronics fails, our name is always going to be connected to a failed project."

Susan sat up in her chair. "But that's not fair."

"That's how the game works," Miranda sighed.

"But I thought everything looked good."

"So far it has," Miranda agreed slowly. "We've ensured that their materials were top of the line. The sub-contractors were all inspected and approved by everyone. The assembly is being done here in the States, and they built in enough lead time to get things put together without error. But I think the math on the original plans is off, and when it comes time for the demonstration, it's going to fail."

"So what are you doing to fix it?"

That was another thing she loved about Susan. She had absolute confidence in Miranda's abilities to take care of things. Miranda was pretty sure she would be able to, too. She might hate being in the limelight, but she knew her damn job. However, this one was going to be tough. That was the reason Miranda had been going through her feel-good file, she'd needed a boost. Something to stimulate some ideas.

"I'm doing it. I just sent an e-mail allocating overtime to the quality control department. I want their findings in forty-eight hours. In the meantime, I'm going to ask Riya to give me the names of some mathematicians she would recommend. I'm not going to let this project fail."

"So you're not going to wait for the QC results," Susan chuckled.

"Nope. Let's hope I'm wrong, but I want to have my ducks in a row in case I'm right."

"Which you probably will be. Will the CTO at Lartronics be mad at you?"

"To begin with, he's going to be pissed as hell, then he'll agree to give me his firstborn."

"Great, you won't have to go through childbirth again," Susan winked.

"As long as they arrange it for me to get a damn epidural this time, I'll be fine," Miranda groused. She was still bitter about that.

"Plus our CEO will probably give you a bonus," Susan grinned, "because Lartronics will give us more business."

"There is that," Miranda agreed.

"And will the generals be grateful?" Susan asked.

"If we do our job right, they'll never know. We want them to think they got a pretty package that worked right on the first try, so they have faith in Lartronics and TAID for all subsequent contracts."

Susan grinned. "Makes sense. I'll send Riya to your office when she gets in."

"Thanks."

———

"The pizza should arrive in twenty minutes. It's from Lefty's," Griff said. It was two weeks later, and he knew Miranda was having a big meeting with everyone, including the CTO from Lartronics who had flown in from out of town, as well as a bevy of programmers and her two hotshot mathematicians.

"Grubhub doesn't deliver Lefty's to the Northwest Corridor Technology Center. Trust me, I've tried."

"This is the Wyatt Leed's delivery service."

Miranda didn't know what made her happier. Hearing her husband's sexy voice over the phone after a rough day at work, or the idea of having a supreme pizza from Lefty's.

"You're too good to me."

"I know you're working on something big," he said. "I know it has you in a twist, and whatever I can do to support you, I want to do."

Miranda thought of something, but before she could say anything, Griff was already answering her unasked question.

"There's eight pizzas coming. Susan told me you have a conference room full of people. You'll have everything but the beer."

"You sweet man. I'll do you a solid, I'll even save the receipt and bill it to the company."

"Now we're talking my language." She could hear his grin over the phone.

Hell, she'd been planning to send Susan out for Subway, but instead they were getting a feast.

She scanned the spreadsheets and schematics in front of her, and was surprised when Susan pinged her.

"That was fast," she said as she picked up her phone. "I didn't think it would get here so quick."

"Want me to bring it in?" Susan asked.

"No, set it up in the conference room. I'll be right in."

"You want your flowers put in the conference room?"

"Huh?" Miranda rubbed her forehead. "What are you talking about, Susan?" But she was talking to a dial tone.

Susan opened the door and walked in with a bouquet of sunflowers in a red vase.

"It's your secret admirer again," Susan said with a questioning smile. "Still no card. I'm telling you, Griff is the most romantic man in the world." Susan put her hand over her forehead, pretending to swoon.

Miranda forced a smile. "Susan, can you do me a favor?" she asked before her friend could put them on her credenza.

"Sure, what?"

"Could you put them someplace else? The last time they gave me a terrible sinus headache. I'd normally suggest you just keep them on your desk, but I know that I'd smell them there too, and it would just be too overwhelming."

"Oh, God, Miranda, does it trigger your migraines? Holy Moly, let me get them out of here. You need to tell Griff. He's going to feel terrible." She practically ran out the door with the bouquet. Miranda couldn't be happier.

That bastard. The mean and evil bastard. How dare he try to worm his way into her life. He was dead. Didn't he get it? He was dead and buried and that's where he needed to stay. Her mind wound backwards to that horrible night. She remembered everything. Every detail.

She tried to shove it down deep, but she couldn't. It roiled around incessantly, and she couldn't focus. She was having trouble seeing the papers on her desk. It seemed to be swimming in front of her eyes.

Miranda picked up her mechanical pencil but it dropped out of her hand. She whimpered.

No! This couldn't be happening. Not this fast.

She blindly reached for her purse, because lights were beginning to pop before her eyes. She fumbled for her top drawer, and found her purse. Her fingers grasped the nasal spray bottle with the migraine medicine, and she immediately took a hit.

She kept her eyes closed, but the light still filtered through her lids. It was excruciating. She would not let the dragon win. She would not! She was better than this. She could beat it. How long did she wait for the medicine to take effect? Finally, she went to grab her desk phone. She knocked over the handset and gave up trying to press the right button.

"Susan," she yelled weakly.

She didn't think she waited long, but it must have been, because she woke to a cool compress on her brow and at the back of her neck, and the lights were out. She felt like she could breathe.

Thank God for Susan and that medicine.

"How long?" she croaked out.

"Long enough for half of the Lefty's pizza to have been eaten," Susan said. Her voice was wobbly.

"Shit."

"Griff is on his way over."

"Susan, that wasn't necessary." She sat up straighter

in her chair, then swallowed a few times, and breathed through her nose. Funny how the thought of Lefty's no longer held any appeal.

She swallowed and it tasted like vomit.

"Are you kidding me? Three-hundred-and-sixty-four days out of the year you scare me a hell of a lot more than Griff. But when it comes to your health, he scares the bejesus out of me. I'm surprised he isn't here by now."

"It was just a headache."

"Headache my ass. This is the fourth time Griff's sent you those flowers in the last twelve months. Why have you never told me that you were so allergic?"

Well, that was the million dollar question. How could she tell Susan that she was allergic to the flowers because a man everyone thought was dead, was sending them instead of Griff?

What was his deal sending the flowers, anyway? It was about damn time she pulled up her big girl panties and found out, instead of acting like a scared four-year-old.

"They say that you can develop an allergy, and that's what happened to me," Miranda lied. "This time it was really bad."

"I'll say," Susan agreed.

Miranda's office door swung open. Griff gave her a steely-eyed look as he took her in. He looked ferocious.

"Miranda, why did you come to work today if a migraine was blooming?" he demanded as he stalked across the room, then knelt down in front of Miranda. He took the cloth from Susan's hand and kept it pressed to her forehead, his other hand cupped Miranda's cheek.

"Oh, Baby, I need to get you home."

"Where's Livvie?" she asked weakly.

"I dropped her off at Dex and Kenna's. She's spending the night."

"Kenna's pregnant. We can't do that to her," Miranda objected.

"Yes we can, they've been buying all the baby shit. I gave them her diaper bag, they're good. Now I'm taking you home." He was like granite. She was going to have to proceed carefully to get her way. She cut her eyes to Susan who rushed out of the office.

"Honey, this meeting is critical."

"You passed out."

"I didn't pass out. I was awake, just really out of it."

"Susan called me from your phone. Do you remember that?"

She looked him straight in the eye. "Yes."

His hands clamped down on the arms of her chair and boxed her in. "You're lying," he growled.

She glared at him. "Prove it."

He continued to stare at her.

"Griff, this is one of the most important meetings of the project," she enunciated clearly. It was her way of admitting that she'd lied, and trying to get him to come around to her way of thinking.

He blew out a breath through gritted teeth.

"Miranda, these migraines are serious," he said in a choked whisper. "We've been to the doctor. You know because you have migraines with auras you're more susceptible to having a stroke. Don't do this to me. Don't do this to Livvie."

She put her hand on his cheek. "I haven't had a migraine in six months. I've even been doing yoga. I'm going to be fine."

"This project is a lot of pressure," he said softly. His concern was so clear. Miranda couldn't tell him what the real reason was. She just wanted that to go away, and she was going to *make* it go away. For all everyone knew, there was nobody named Roger Heinrich, and he was going to remain a dead nobody.

"You can wait for me here in the office, I'll keep the meeting to just three hours. How's that?"

Griff got a mutinous expression on his face.

Shit, she wasn't going to win.

Then it came to her. "You trust Riya, don't you?"

"Huh? What does Riya have to do with anything?"

"Move," Miranda pushed him out of her way so she could reach for her cell phone. She punched in Riya's number.

"Riya, I need a favor. I know you're not working on the Helios project, but you have a top secret clearance, and Griff trusts you. Can you come to my office as soon as possible and sit in on a meeting with me?"

Riya paused on the other end. "What's the dress code?"

"Anything you want, just get here," Miranda answered.

Riya hung up.

Miranda was too wiped out to laugh, otherwise she would. That was her friend the scientist. She had her question answered and was on her way, no need for chit chat. Riya Patel was one of the most brilliant minds on the planet, but she had almost no social skills. Miranda absolutely adored the woman, and was thankful every day that she was part of her team.

"As soon as Riya gets here, we'll tell her about the migraine and what to monitor me for, and she can sit in on the meeting. How does that sound? I'd have you come in, but you're not cleared for it."

Griff opened his mouth.

"Please, Griff." If he disagreed, she'd acquiesce. He'd never asked her to make a choice like this before. He really had a good reason to ask for it in his opinion, and unless she came clean as to what the real stressor was, she was stuck.

"Do you promise to bail if Riya so much as raises an eyebrow?" he eventually asked.

"Hell, knowing her, once we explain the situation, she'll stop the meeting and drag my ass out if she thinks there's an issue."

He cocked his head. "Good point."

10

IT HAD TAKEN EVERYTHING MIRANDA COULD DO TO PUT Griff off the previous night. He'd wanted to talk, but she'd insisted the migraine had wiped her out. He'd been great making breakfast, going out and putting gas in her SUV, and taking Livvie to the Little Handprints Daycare this morning. She didn't deserve him. She got into work at ten a.m., knowing the dreaded blocked call would be coming. It always did after the flowers.

Loathing coated her tongue, making her gag as the phone rang. But she was going to finish this, once and for all. He was not going to steal her honor. Not anymore.

"Let's get this over with." she answered.

"Is that any way to greet your father?"

"Heinrich, what do you want? You're barely hanging on at DHS, just one more fuck-up and they're going to boot your ass. You're behind two mortgage payments, and your third wife left you. Rumor has it you miss the yippy dog she took with her. Your life is shit." She waited a beat for emphasis. "As it should be. I'll give you a tip, you can't afford to be sending me flowers. You probably can't even afford the blocked number upgrade on your phone. So what do you want?"

"Randa—" his voice was sickly sweet.

"Don't call me that," she cut him off, her voice ice. That nickname was reserved for Hope.

"I see you've been doing your homework. Had one of your husband's little SEAL buddies look me up?"

"Could be," she answered noncommittally. She wasn't going to admit to a damn thing, but if he thought she wasn't capable of finding out about his pathetic little life, he was sorely mistaken. Granted, she did end up tapping a friend of hers who had quit TAID and opened her own cyber-security company, but still, a lot of the stuff she'd discovered on her own.

"Still, it's nice to have this much of a conversation with you, normally you just hang up."

He was right. Eleven months ago when she'd gotten the first arrangement of sunflowers in the red vase, she'd gotten a call from the blocked number and picked up. Then she'd heard his voice and ice dripped down her spine. She'd immediately hung up. He'd called until she'd powered off her phone. Bastard had never left a voice mail, thank God.

"What are you talking about, Heinrich? We had a conversation when you hunted me down three years ago."

"Can't you find it in your heart to call me dad?" he wheedled.

Miranda almost choked at the very thought. "You're lucky my mother raised me to be so polite, otherwise I wouldn't be calling you Heinrich."

"Yeah, Olivia was quite a woman, wasn't she?"

Miranda slammed the flat of her hand on her desk. "Don't you dare say her name."

"I was paying her a compliment," he whined.

"If you want this conversation to continue, Heinrich, you will never say her name again, are we clear?"

There was no response.

"Answer me."

"Can't you at least call me Roger?" His voice grated on her nerves.

Dammit, he was a bellyacher. She hated that.

"Heinrich, what do you want?" She enunciated every word clearly.

"I just want to spend time with you. Is that so hard to believe?"

She vaguely remembered him saying the same thing to her when she'd been at Griff's house three years ago. She'd replayed that time in her head, and realized that he must have staked out Griff's duplex and waited for her nurse to leave before approaching.

"What do you want?" She repeated her question, her voice was flat.

Had she asked him that question three years ago, or had she been grateful to see him? It killed her that the conversation with him was still fuzzy around the edges. He'd visited her at Griff's house, right after she'd taken pain medication. He must have been keeping track of her schedule, because he came between the time when Griff left in the morning and before her nurse, Lilah arrived. So when her father had kept knocking on the door, she was totally out of it.

Before getting pictures from Ellen's cyber-security company, Miranda just had a dim shadow of Roger Heinrich's face seen through Griff's screen door. She remembered him praising her for saving Hope. Vaguely, she remembered him gushing a lot about how wonderful she was.

Now it disgusted her to realize that deep down it had once been her heart's secret desire that he love her, and there he'd been, giving it to her. Miranda remembered crying at Griff's door, and it was when her father had tried to open the door and hug her, that all hell broke loose. She wasn't a four-year-old wishing that her daddy loved her. She might be concussed and drugged but she remembered this was the bastard who'd belted and kicked her mom and railed at her for not having 'aborted the thing'. Telling her mom that the brat should never have been born.

Miranda didn't even remember closing the door, but she had a memory of Lilah finding her slumped on the couch and worrying about why she wasn't in bed. By the time Griff got home that night, it was as if it had all been a horrible dream.

"Answer me," she bit out again, back in the present. "What the hell do you want? Is it money? Because you're not going to get a cent."

"I just want to see my sweet girl."

"So your brilliant idea has been to send me creepy

flowers, to try to get me to see you, huh? I don't believe you. You want something, and it's not going to happen."

"Miranda," he sputtered. "You're getting it all wrong. I've been trying to establish a relationship with you from the very beginning. You broke my heart when you threw me out of that SEAL's house three years ago. I saw how upset you were, I never wanted that. That's why I left you alone for two years."

Why in the hell was she even listening to this drivel? Oh yeah, because she wanted him out of her life once and for all so there'd be no more secrets.

"Just tell me what I have to do to make you dead to me like you were for the first twenty-eight years of my life, Heinrich."

"Can't you at least call me Roger?"

"No," she snapped out.

"I need to see you. This isn't something I feel comfortable talking about over the phone."

"There is no way I'm going to meet with some monster from my past who sends me threatening flowers, and calls me from a blocked number. Just tell me what you want, so I can scrape you off my shoe, once and for all."

"So there is no way I can get you to relent? No way I can appeal to your better nature?"

Was he serious?

"I want you out of my life. For twenty-eight years, you've been dead to me. I want those blissful days back. Crawl back under your rock. If I call you Roger, will you go?"

"Angel, I don't believe you. I think you do care."

Roger Heinrich's voice had changed, he sounded more confident. "You would do a lot of things for me. You taking the time to have me investigated, and taking this call, proves it."

"Think you're kind of smart, huh? All that proves, is that I want to analyze all the bugs that crawl out from underneath the rocks near me. Low and behold, your shell is one of the most fragile I've ever come across."

"When did you get so allergic to sunflowers, Angel?"

Miranda felt her breath saw out of her lungs. She had trouble taking in the next one. Her mind scrambled to think of who in the TAID building would have been aware of her sudden *allergy* to the flowers she'd received.

Her head swiveled around, looking at the window that showed a beautiful cloudless blue sky. Her office couldn't be bugged, it was swept for surveillance equipment twice a week.

"I can hear you breathing hard. Be careful, I would hate for you to trigger another migraine."

She hung up the phone.

It was two o'clock. She grabbed her purse and marched out of her office. Susan looked up, startled.

"Where are you headed?"

"Heading home. Call me if anything pops up."

Susan looked like she wanted to ask another question, but she ignored her as she walked by the receptionist's desk and headed for the elevator. Griff was at base. She was headed to the daycare to pick up

Livvie. She needed to see her daughter, and take her home. How in the hell had that monster known what the fuck was going on in her office?

How had he known?

Her shoulder hurt. That's when she realized she was pulling on her purse so hard that the shoulder strap was digging a deep groove into her flesh.

Think, Slade. Think.

She was on the fourteenth floor. Second from the top. The entire building was filled with TAID employees. The technology center had eight buildings and TAID took up three of them. Even with thirty-two hundred people, the rumor mill was rife with petty gossip. Hell, she would bet her bottom dollar that at least fifty people knew that she and Griff were trying to have another baby, maybe even as many as a hundred knew.

So if Susan gave away her flowers to some lucky employee because she had an allergy, that little nugget of information could have gotten to any number of people. But what about the migraine?

She surged out of the elevator and rushed to her cross-over SUV. She drove within the speed limit to get to Livvie's daycare. By the time she got there, she was breathing normally and thinking rationally. She'd blown this out of proportion. Heinrich had just used a dumb little DHS trick and found out a tiny bit of useless information about her. Still...

"Who's my good girl?" Miranda asked as she buckled her daughter into her car seat.

Livvie giggled. Miranda knew it was probably because of the toy giraffe she gave her daughter more than her teasing. She hopped back into the driver's seat and touched the connection to her phone, dialing her friend, Ellen.

"Hey, Miranda. What's up?"

"Remember that guy Roger Heinrich I had you check out?"

"Sure."

"The first order of business is that you need to cash the check I sent."

"Not going to happen," Ellen laughed. "You were my mentor at TAID, there isn't a chance in hell I'm going to take your money."

Miranda knew it was a losing battle. "Fine, but this time I want you to cash it, because I need more info."

She heard Ellen's chair squeak. "What's up?"

Miranda needed to tread carefully. Ellen was bright. So far she hadn't asked any questions, she'd just taken Miranda at face value. But if she thought she was in trouble, she'd start pressing her.

"I just think there's a little bit more than meets the eye," Miranda said casually.

"Can you be more specific? Is it about his job?"

She should have figured she would zero in on the topic.

"Got it in one. He seems to be a little more plugged-in than I originally suspected."

"Miranda, is he a threat to you?"

The giraffe landed on the passenger seat in front of

her. She had about two minutes before Livvie would let loose.

"Nah."

"Who is he to you?"

Miranda pulled up to the stop sign two blocks from her house. She looked to her left and tried to come up with something plausible, and failed.

"Ellen, can I ask a solid?"

"You're not going to tell me, are you? How much trouble are you in? What does he have over you?"

Miranda scraped out the best sounding laugh she could. "Ellen, your imagination is out of control. He has nothing over me. Nothing at all. If I thought he was a threat, I'd tell you and pull in Griff. I promise you."

There was a long pause. "Dammit, Miranda, you'd better. If I find out anything that points to him having a proverbial gun to your head, all bets are off, got it?"

"Hell yeah." And she meant it. She had far too much to lose to be stupid. "I just need you to dig a little deeper. There's more going on than just him being a deadbeat. He actually has a brain. I want to know what his job was at the DHS. Was it always the same thing? Did he have anything to do with Intelligence?"

"I'm not liking this."

"I promise you, Ellen, I'll call you and let you know if anything hinky is going on. In the meantime, can you make this a priority?"

Her friend took a while to answer. "Of course I'll make it a priority. But if one flag comes up, I'm flying in from Denver."

"I wouldn't expect anything else," Miranda put a

smile into her voice. "I'll talk to you later." She disconnected the call and hit her steering wheel. "Dammit!"

Livvie let out a startled cry.

"Sorry, Baby Girl. Mommy didn't mean to be loud."

11

GRIFF QUIETLY UNLOCKED THE FRONT DOOR. HE HADN'T parked in their garage, because the sound of the door going up would have alerted Miranda that he'd come home early, too. After last night maybe his wife was actually taking care of herself. She'd scared the hell out of him with her migraine. Something was definitely up. He'd seen her work on hellish projects before, but they'd never put this kind of stress on her. He'd bet his bottom dollar it wasn't because they wanted to have another baby, that had been her idea.

No, there was something going on, and he was going to get to the bottom of it.

Chill. Quit being a paranoid fuck.

As he closed the door behind him, he heard little girl giggles and then he heard older girl giggles. It warmed his heart, and he went down the short hallway and turned the corner. All of the dining room chairs were in the living room, the coffee table had been shoved aside, and two sheets were strung out between the chairs and the couch. He could see his little girl's head pressed against the inside of the sheet.

"Careful Livvie, or the ceiling might fall down again," Miranda said gently.

His adventurous little girl wormed her head through the connection point of the two sheets and grinned when she saw him.

"Dada," she cried out, then giggled. She motioned for him to come into the fort.

"Griff?" Miranda scrambled out from under the sheets. "What the heck are you doing home?"

"I heard there was a blanket fort at the Porter residence, and I didn't want to miss out." He gave her a quick kiss and Livvie emerged with her arms out.

"Up Dada." He swung her up in his arms and gave her a kiss.

"Down," she said pointing to the floor. Both adults laughed as she quickly crawled back under the sheets. Then she poked her head out again. "Want smores."

"That's your fault," Miranda said. "And if you give in, you have to deal with the sugar high."

Griff did a mental inventory of the kitchen and realized they were out of marshmallows. "If I go to the store, what would you want me to pick up for dinner?" he asked.

"You are such a soft touch. You're going to make her S-M-O-R-E-S," she spelled out.

Griff chose to believe that it was getting warm in the house and he was not blushing. SEALs did not blush.

Miranda laughed.

"Besides, I feel like cooking," he defended himself. "So what should I get from the store?"

"Chef gets to decide."

"Store?" Livvie said as she crawled out back out of the fort. She looked up at Griff. Riding in the grocery cart was one of her favorite things.

"That's right, Munchkin, I'm going to the store. Want to go with me?" he asked.

"Store!" she crowed. She sped out of the living room toward her bedroom. His kid was a runner.

"I'm thinking I should leave this up, what do you think? Smores in a fort sounds like a treat, right?" Miranda went to straighten the sheets.

"Definitely," Griff agreed as he helped. "So what made you decide to leave work early? You weren't getting a migraine, were you?"

She looked up at him and gave him a reassuring smile. "Nope, nothing like that. I just needed some family time. Friday's the big meeting and I'm thinking I might need a sleeping bag at the office."

"That's not funny." Griff stared at her.

"I'm kidding," she smiled.

"I'm serious, Miranda. You need your sleep. You have a perfectly fine home office. Don't make me go Neanderthal on your ass and drag you home."

He watched a myriad of emotions cross her face until finally she relented. "You're right. My days of one hundred and twenty hour work weeks are long gone."

"Damn right they are, you're a Porter now."

"Didn't Dex mention something about you going

thirty-two hours straight when you were in a sniper position?" Miranda asked sweetly.

He was going to kill his teammate.

"Store!"

They turned when Livvie came out holding her socks and one shoe.

Saved by the bell.

MIRANDA BIT into her second smore of the night as she sat in front of her computer. The dinner and dessert she'd had with Livvie and Griff in the fort five hours ago had long worn off, and now that they were both asleep she could get busy. She opened her work e-mail and downloaded the encrypted file titled Pegasus. The project was for a highly-advanced ghost bomber that was undetectable by any radar that had yet to be devised. The cherry on top was that it was green screen technology which allowed it to act like a chameleon with its surroundings and was barely discernable to the naked eye. The reason it was referred to as Pegasus was a nod to Wonder Woman's invisible jet, which had been created when they transformed the winged horse into the super hero's plane.

After a couple of hours poring over spreadsheets and schematics, she got up from her desk and rubbed her lower back. She took her empty plate into the kitchen and poured some marshmallows into a bowl and debated whether she wanted a cola or milk.

Looking at the clock on the microwave, she went for the milk.

As she sat down in her chair, she almost dropped her bowl when her phone dinged.

"Dammit."

She'd forgotten that she'd taken it off the night time mode in case the Lartronics CTO wanted to get in touch with her. *Maybe she should have gone for the cola.* Evan Banks probably wanted her take on the file he sent. She picked up her phone.

Rage shot through her. It was a text from that damned blocked number. She resisted the urge to throw her phone across the room. She was an adult, for God's sake. She took a deep breath. She had a mega shit-ton of work to get done. She could not and would not deal with this now.

Carefully placing the phone upside down on her desk, she went back to focusing on the files on her computer screen. When it got to the point that she couldn't concentrate anymore, she powered down and called it a night. She might, just might, have made a rude gesture at her phone before turning off her desk lamp.

When she got to the bedroom, her husband she stopped short when she found Griff up reading a book. This was not normal.

"Hey," she smiled.

"ARE there any marshmallows left in the kitchen?" he asked.

Ease into it.

She gave him a quizzical glance. "Not buying it, Porter. What's on your mind?"

"Maybe I want some fluffy goodness," he teased.

She yawned, "Tell you what, I'm going to the bathroom and changing for bed. You get your thoughts together, or grab the last of the marshmallows if you're so inclined, and we'll meet back here? Is it a deal?"

God, she looked exhausted.

"Just two more days and the presentation is finished, right?" he said as she peeled out of her sweater and went to the dresser to take off her earrings.

"Right."

His wife was a tough nut to crack, but last night had scared the shit out of him. It was time for a 'Come to Jesus' meeting. He'd been on the receiving end of a few in their time together, but she hadn't.

For God's sake, it had taken him three weeks after bringing her home from the hospital before she would admit that she couldn't remember a lot of things. His woman held things close to her chest. After three years together, he'd realized a lot of it was due to how she'd been raised. She'd learned her to keep of cone of silence at her mother's knee. Olivia had been a single woman who'd been left pregnant by some dead asshole, so she didn't trust anyone.

Of course that wasn't the way Miranda told the story.

Nope, Miranda's version was way the hell different.

She talked about a happy shiny childhood, where she and her mom did everything together and they were one another's best friends. But Griff read that as isolated. Miranda also explained how her mother always made sure she was cared for and provided Miranda with everything she needed. Griff easily discerned that meant Miranda rarely, if ever, got the things a little girl *wanted*. Yeah, she had an warm apartment, clothes, food and braces, but there were no extracurricular activities for little Miranda. She didn't get to go to camp with her friends.

Nope, it was her and Olivia Slade against the world. In some ways, Miranda still felt that way and Griff felt like he was still breaking down those barriers.

He got out of the bed and followed into the master bath. "Let me run you a bath."

"I'm fine with a shower," she said in a tired voice.

He plugged the tub and started the water running. He poured in the bath salts that she liked.

"Is this about last night's migraine?"

"And you working on your computer for five hours tonight."

"Only four and a half," she protested.

"Five."

"You're intent on pampering me, huh?" She sat down on the side of the bathtub.

"I'm giving it my best shot."

"What's wrong?"

"That's my line." Griff winced when he heard how hard that came out.

"Honey, I'm sorry I worried you. I didn't mean to."

"And therein lies the problem," he sighed. "You know, leaning on me isn't a crime."

She drew back and searched his face. "What are you talking about? I lean on you all the time."

Griff used the biggest gun in his arsenal and stayed silent.

"I do. I lean on you a lot," she insisted. "I miss you like hell when you're on a mission, and when you come back, I practically fall into your arms."

"Miranda, why don't you wake me up when you have nightmares?"

She turned her face and looked into the rising water. "I told you, I don't remember those."

He would have called her a liar again, but he couldn't stomach it. It hurt. They were three years into their marriage, they had a child together, and she still didn't share the things that hurt her.

Fuck silence.

"Wouldn't it feel better to share what's hurting you?" he ground out.

She turned back to him, and her eyes were wet. "I love you more than I've ever loved anybody in my life, besides Livvie. I trust you more than I've ever trusted anybody in my life. I know you don't believe me, Griffin, but it's true. But there's just some things that I need to work out on my own."

He looked at her. Looked deep in her eyes. He pulled her hand and placed it over his heart. "You have to trust me. This isn't just you and me, this is Livvie. This is the child you might be carrying right now. I need you to dig deep. I know it hurts. I know it's scary. I know it goes against all of your beliefs to trust that I'll love you no matter what. That'll I'll never go away. But I won't. Even if I get angry, I won't go away. Even if I'm pissed as hell, I'm going to love you until the earth crumbles. I'm going to love you past forever."

Her lip trembled.

"You can't."

"I will, Baby," he said hoarsely.

He watched as tears welled in her beautiful blue eyes.

"It's bad." She looked down, her voice faltering. "I'm bad. I should never have been born."

His gut clenched.

What was she going to say? Could he handle it?

"You're not bad. You're the best thing that's ever happened to me. I adore you. Tell me, I'm your safe place."

Soft, fat tears fell.

He turned off the water, and pulled them both to the floor so they rested against the tub. "Tell me, Baby."

"I need your help. I thought I could make him go away. I thought I could handle it by myself. He's my problem."

"We're a team. I *always* have your back. Who's harassing you."

Who did he have to kill?

"Roger Heinrich." She tried to pull out of his arms. "I hate him. He's a no good bastard. He hit mom. He said I needed to be aborted. He's the one who sent those goddamn flowers. He's poison."

Her words ran together.

Hit her mom?

"Miranda, who is he to you?"

"He's the one who abandoned mom all those years ago. He found me three years ago after the train wreck, but I kicked him to the curb." This time when she tried to get up, he released her. Miranda started to walk the length the bathroom.

"I must have been four when he came to our house in Ohio. I watched from the top of the stairs. It's burned into my memory. He screamed at Mom that she should have aborted the brat. Then he hit her and kicked her. He told her never to contact him again. It was years later that I found out what the word aborted meant."

Griff zeroed in on the pertinent facts. "What do you mean he contacted you three years ago? Was this after we met?"

"It was when I was staying at your house, I barely remember the confrontation. I got rid of him. I thought it was for good."

Griff surged up from the floor. "Why didn't you tell me?"

She looked up at him confused. It was clear she'd been lost in her own memories as she'd told her story. "Because this bastard was my problem. I hardly knew you. Why would I tell you?"

"How about because I was the man who loved you?"

He saw the confused look on her face. Shit, the thought really hadn't been on her radar.

Chill the fuck out, Porter.

She rested her hands on his chest, "Griff, I'm sorry, it just-"

He sighed. "It's all right. I get it. Now tell me what's going on."

———

GRIFF FINALLY GOT Miranda to bed. She'd been emotionally wiped out. Part of him had wanted to crawl in with her, hold and comfort her and assure her that everything was good now that she'd told him about Heinrich.

Then there was the part that wanted to punch holes in the walls because she'd been targeted, going through this alone *and hadn't fucking told him!*

And finally, there was the part of him that had had his ass up all night at the desk. Miranda had told him about hiring Ellen Fairfax, and that was his first call, even though it was three o'clock in the morning in Denver.

She'd made a little progress since talking to Miranda the previous day, managing to dig up an old teammate of Heinrich's who had been fired from DHS, who had been willing to dish some dirt on the man. Apparently there were rumors of Heinrich doing favors with one of the cartels down in Mexico, but nothing could be proven. His actual write-up, and what he would likely be fired for, was gross incompetence.

Ellen also had calls out to his last two ex-wives. The first one had gone off the grid, which was not a good sign. Heinrich's last known address was Phoenix Arizona. Ellen had actually flown out there three days ago and knocked on doors. Nobody had seen him for weeks.

"I don't have a good feeling about this, Griff."

He wanted to rail at her, but he'd only met the woman once at a company picnic. She was Miranda's friend and had no real ties to him. "From now on, I need you to report in to *both* Miranda and I, do you understand?"

"Miranda's the one paying for my services."

"That's a bunch of horseshit. You're not cashing her checks. Now, if you want to be blackballed by some of the best cyber-security people in the business, I can arrange that, or if you want to have the backing of these guys, it's all up to you. But don't try to play fucking hardball with me when it comes to my wife and kid."

"Hey, hey, hey. I really wasn't trying to play hardball. But Miranda comes first. As long as she's cool, I'm cool. No matter what, her health and well-being are my number one priority. I have never doubted that you have her back."

Griff blew out a long breath. "Sorry, I overreacted. Long night."

"Look, this guy is a tool. He doesn't have a chance against you and yours. Okay?" Ellen assured him.

Griff rubbed the back of his neck. "That's my take, too. But I don't want to take any chances."

"You've got this."

"Thanks." He disconnected.

MIRANDA LOOKED over at her husband. God, she'd married a good one. He glanced over at her, took one of his hands off the steering wheel, then grabbed her hand.

"Thank you."

He didn't pretend to not know what she was talking about. He brought her hand to his mouth and kissed it. "You're welcome. Thank you for finally trusting me. I know it was hard."

Miranda snorted, then sighed. Anybody else she'd tell them to get their ass to counselling. Luckily they'd handled the shit last night, got past it, and now she'd just have to deal with an over protective SEAL of a husband until Daddy Dearest was gone for good.

"So you remember the deal, right?"

"Yes, Sir. You're in charge. First you dropped off Livvie, now you're dropping me off. Then after you're done with the tadpoles, you'll pick Livvie up, feed her dinner, drop her off at Kenna and Dex's and come pick me up."

"Damn right. You don't leave the building without me. If there's a problem, I will send one of the team to get you. Got it?"

After all the bullshit she'd put him through, there wasn't a chance in hell she was going to tell him it was overkill. She wasn't. He was coming late into this game, it was his right to protect her, he needed this, even if he was going *way* over the top.

Keep your mouth shut Miranda.

"Griff, both you and Ellen agree that he's a gnat on a dog's ass."

"Miranda, he knew that the flowers made you allergic and that you got a migraine. He's got eyes and ears in your building. This is serious shit. We're taking this seriously. Got it?"

"Yes, Sir."

"Dammit, we discussed that too. I'm not an officer," he said as he pulled up to the front of the building. "Don't call me Sir." Then he relented and waggled his eyebrows. "Unless we're in the bedroom."

She burst out laughing.

She loved this man.

12

"MIRANDA, YOU LOOK LIKE YOU GOT LUCKY. YOU'RE wearing a shit-eating grin, but you have bags under your eyes. So was it a late night?" Susan asked as she sat down in front of her desk.

"It *was* a late night. And it turns out I scored big time in the husband lottery."

"Hell, we both did," Susan grinned. "So, do we have to work double time today on the project because you were indulging in sexy-time instead of working?"

"Nope, I got a lot done on that front, too." Miranda beamed. "And...there's good news. Everything I reviewed looked good. There was only one thing of any significance that the QC department found, and it correlated with Riya's mathematician. Evan, the CTO from Lartronics, should be calling any time now."

"That's why I'm here. He's not going to call. He should be here in three hours. He took the red-eye."

Miranda's eyes shot over to her computer screen.

She perused her e-mail and didn't see any notices that the CTO was planning on coming to San Diego.

What the hell?

"How'd you find out?"

Susan's smile got wide. "I have an *in* with his assistant. She keeps me abreast of his schedule when it pertains to TAID."

"How'd you manage that?" Miranda asked.

"I told her I always wanted to have the kind of snacks he likes on hand whenever he visits."

"Oh, you're sneaky," Miranda beamed. "In that case, do me a favor and arrange to have everybody here for a meeting this afternoon. I want to do a debrief after I talk to Evan."

"Sounds good. Anything else?"

"Nope. I want to start working on my summary," she said as she pulled out her laptop from her computer bag.

"I'll leave you to it."

Miranda was soon writing up bullet points.

Her phone sounded with an incoming text. When she looked down, she realized an hour and a half had gone by.

Shit! She'd forgotten all about the text she'd received last night from the blocked number. What an idiot! She should have told Griff.

When she saw the new one was from Scarlett Hale, she figured Daddy Dearest could wait five more minutes. She deserved something sweet.

"Miranda, I didn't expect you to call me during your

busy work day." Miranda loved listening to the older woman's enthusiastic voice.

"You mentioned brunch in your text. That required an immediate response. What did you have in mind?"

"I was talking to your mother-in-law, she needs a baby fix. Claudia was thinking she could come down this way and all of us could go to brunch on Sunday. What do you think?"

Miranda sighed. "Is there any way we could postpone for one week? This Friday is a deliverable from hell. All I want to do this weekend is crawl into bed and sleep."

"That would actually be even better because Gianna will be in town."

Miranda perked up. She'd never met Scarlett's daughter. She'd heard about her, but never met her. "Maybe some of Griff's sisters could be talked into coming, too. We could make it a real event."

"Claudia would love that." Miranda heard the excitement in Scarlett's voice. "If you're neck deep in work, how about if I arrange it all?"

"I would love that, are you sure you don't mind?"

"Positive. I'll just tell you where you have to be the day before."

It was great dealing with organized women. "Thanks. That'll be a great way to celebrate the project milestone."

"Okay, well I'll leave you to it. Bye," Scarlett said just before she hung up.

Miranda immediately clicked over to the other text. It had an attachment.

My granddaughter is beautiful.

The hair on the back of her neck raised.

Miranda's thumb swiped on her screen. It took a long moment for her to comprehend what she was seeing. It looked so normal. There was Livvie like she had seen her plenty of times before, sitting in the grocery store shopping cart, holding onto her stuffed giraffe with one hand, and the cart's handle with the other. Griff's back muscles were well-defined in his T-shirt as he reached up to a shelf for a can of something.

Livvie was wearing her little yellow outfit from yesterday.

Wait a minute. This picture had been taken when Griff had gone to the store with her last evening!

Now the picture was going out of focus.

No, wait, her hand was trembling.

The phone vibrated again.

Blocked caller.

Bastard!

Her eyes flashed upwards. Her door was closed.

"You tagged your message, didn't you?" she hissed into the phone. "What do you want?"

"It took you long enough to open it. Anyway, can't a man just take pride in his flesh and blood. I can't believe you've denied me a chance to meet my granddaughter. She's really lovely, Miranda." Butter wouldn't melt in his mouth.

"This isn't fun and games anymore. You can have me on a string as much as you want. But my daughter? You've crossed a line. We're through. I'm calling the police."

"And tell them what, exactly?" he asked smoothly. "I haven't done one thing wrong. All I've done is try to establish a relationship with my daughter."

She hung up.

She forwarded the text to Griff's phone. Before she could then dial Griff, another text came through from the blocked number. It had another attachment. She couldn't open it fast enough. It showed a picture of the exterior of Livvie's daycare. When her phone rang and the blocked number showed again she didn't answer it, because she was dialing the daycare center.

"Answer, answer," she chanted into the phone. On the third ring, they picked up.

"This is Mrs. Porter, Livvie Porter's mom," she blurted out as soon as she heard the person answer the phone.

"What?"

Miranda didn't recognize the voice.

She took a breath and then repeated herself.

"How may I help you, Mrs. Porter?"

"I'm going to be there in a twenty or thirty minutes. Please only release my daughter to her father Griffin or to me. Please ensure that both of us provide our identification."

Dammit, how was she going to get there? She didn't have her SUV.

"Please hold."

"Susan!" she yelled.

Miranda was suddenly confronted by static-y music.

She pushed away from her desk and yanked her

drawer open. She grabbed out her black purse and slung it over her shoulder as she kept her phone to her ear.

"Susan!" she yelled again. When she got to her office door and yanked it open, she and her friend ran into one another.

"What's wrong?" Susan cried. "Is it Livvie? Griff?"

"Livvie. I have to get to the daycare. I need your car."

"I can drive," Susan said. She turned to her desk and fumbled for her bag from under her desk.

"No, just give me your car keys. "Is Hope still using a booster seat?"

"Yep."

"Great. You're in your parking spot?"

"Yeah. Please let me come with you," Susan begged.

"No, I need you here to handle things."

"What's wrong. Is she injured?"

"No, she's not. I'll call you later," she snatched the keys out of Susan's hands and flew through the glass doors at reception and pressed the down arrow at the elevator.

"Miranda? This is April Marsh. Is there some sort of problem I need to be aware of?"

Ah hell, she'd forgotten she'd had the phone to her ear.

"I don't have time, April. Just only release Livvie to Griff or me. Make sure we have ID. I'll explain more when I get there."

She got in the elevator.

"Do I need to call the authorities, or is this a family matter?"

The elevator door closed, cutting off the conversation.

"Dammit!"

Why hadn't Griff called her? She'd forwarded him that text what seemed like twenty minutes ago. But she knew it was only two or three.

Her mind raced. Finally the elevator door opened, but it wasn't to her garage door level, it was the lobby. Nobody got on. She banged on the button but the elevator wouldn't cooperate.

She rushed out of the elevator, down the flight of stairs from the lobby to the garage and went straight to Susan's mini-van.

"Dammit all to hell!" she screamed, as she waited for the seat to push back so her face didn't touch the windshield. As she waited she gave a voice command to her phone to call Griff and it went to voicemail. *How was that possible when they just went over security?*

"Griff, I forwarded you a text from Heinrich. He took a picture of you and Livvie from last night when you were at the grocery store. It's in your phone. Then he sent another pic of Livvie's daycare. I know you told me not to leave the building, but you're too far away in Coronado. I took Susan's car. I'm picking up Livvie and taking her home. You have that place set up like Fort Knox. We'll be safe." She got the seat into position and started the car. "Why the fuck aren't you answering?" she wailed then hung up as she pulled out of the garage.

Her phone beeped, and she glanced down. It was the blocked number.

Play it cool. You have to play it cool. This is Livvie we're talking about.

"Heinrich, you're beginning to annoy me," she said dryly.

"No, I'm beginning to scare you. Now be a good girl and come meet with Daddy."

She pressed her foot down harder on her accelerator, as she came up on the freeway entrance.

"I've called the police," she lied. "But then I did worse. You're about to meet your own personal nightmare. And he's going to rain Armageddon down on your ass."

The man chuckled.

A semi-truck in the right hand lane forced her to slow down before she could merge. "Angel, you're reading the situation wrong...again. You think the authorities or your G.I. Joe is going to scare me? Nope. I have bogeymen like you wouldn't believe coming out of the woodwork. You're talking to a desperate man. Do you know what the problem is when you're dealing with someone who's desperate? They have nothing to fear."

She looked up at the green sign on the freeway, her exit was just four and a half more miles. Her hand almost slipped as she went to change lanes again. She switched hands and wiped her sweaty palm against her gray slacks.

"Well then you're just too stupid to live."

She disconnected the call.

She called Griff. It went to voicemail again.

"Fuck," she screamed loudly in the interior of the car.

Two more miles to her exit.

She picked up her phone to call Scarlett so that she could get Josiah to find Griff when it finally dawned on her that Griff had told her what to do. He said it was something that Dex had recently put into place for all team members and their women. It was some kind of techie SOS that was now set up on everybody's phones.

Please God, let it work.

She texted 505 to Griff's phone. He had promised that no matter what, somebody from one of the teams would always be monitoring this and would call them back.

Her phone rang, and she didn't recognize the number. She answered it.

"Miranda? This is Kane McNamara. I'm Dex Evan's communication counterpoint on the Night Storm SEAL team out in Virginia. How bad is it?"

"I need my husband. I don't know how bad it is." She saw her white knuckles on the steering wheel and she forced herself not to cry in fear and frustration. "My estranged father is DHS, he's taken pictures of my daughter. She's almost two." She choked back a gasp just thinking about it.

"I'm listening." There was a click on the line.

"Who's on the phone?" Griff demanded.

"Griff! It's me."

"This is McNamara with Night Storm. Miranda was just explaining how her father has been taking pictures of your daughter and threatening her. You're worried for her safety, is that right Miranda?"

"Yes." Miranda sped up to whiz through the yellow light.

"Why didn't you answer your phone?" Miranda demanded.

"I'll get someone to the daycare," Griff said steadily.

"I'm on my way there now." She honked her horn at the car that decided to take a right from the left hand turn lane.

"Why aren't you at your office?" Griff roared.

"I'm here at the daycare."

Miranda parked in the teacher-of-the-year parking spot at the front and slammed out of the car. Her phone fell into the footwell of the passenger seat. She could hear Griff still yelling. She grabbed her purse since she was going to need her identification.

13

"MIRANDA!" GRIFF SHOUTED INTO THE PHONE. IT WAS NO use, she wasn't answering. This was un-fucking-acceptable.

"Kane, get her back on the line!" Griff shouted above the pounding of the surf. He was on the beach in Coronado near the BUD/S Grinder.

"Porter, the line's still open. She's just not talking."

"Griff." He shrugged off the hand on his shoulder.

"Griff, listen to me." He twisted and shoved Dex's hand away.

"What?" he roared. He wanted to yell loud enough for heaven to hear. Hell, it sounded like there was a roaring in his head right now. It was as if an ordinance had gone off beside his ear, and he was dealing with the percussion.

Livvie.

He scrolled through the numbers listed in his phone. Then realized it wasn't his phone, it was Dex's. Dammit, he needed the number to the Little

Handprints Daycare. God, that log must have landed on him harder than he'd realized. *Goddamn tadpoles!* Not only had the log they'd been supposed to be carrying landed on him, it had busted his phone. Dex had been steering him toward the base medic because his friend thought he might have a busted rib.

How long since Miranda stopped talking?

"Not even three minutes," Dex said. Griff must have asked the question aloud.

"What's your passcode?" he demanded of Dex now that the screen was locked.

"What do you need?" Dex asked.

"Little Handprints Daycare," Griff answered.

In a minute, Dex was shoving the phone at him and then he left him.

"Home of Little Handprints," a too-sweet voice answered.

"Is my wife there?" he demanded. "I need to speak to her. I'm looking for Miranda Porter."

"I need to put you on a brief hold, is that all right?"

"No, it's not. Answer my question."

"But I asked you to hold, you were supposed to say yes," the young woman said.

"I said no. Find Miranda."

"Oh. Okay." The receiver clattered and he imagined a startled fairy princess and it pissed him off.

A different voice spoke next. "Who is this?"

Finally, an adult. "This is Griffin Porter. Put my wife on the line. I need to speak to her immediately."

"Griff, this is April Marsh. Miranda just left with Livvie, but I made her show her I.D. as requested. She assured me that the two of you had everything under control."

Griff looked up and saw Dex running back to him. He'd been talking to one of the Instructors who'd been leading the tadpoles on their run. Dex came back with a phone to his ear.

He made a motion with his arm for Griff to follow him.

"April, how long ago did Miranda leave? Was she under any duress?" Griff asked as he started a slow run after Dex. He would have run faster but he wouldn't have been able to hear April.

"Absolutely not. I asked her almost that exact question. It concerned me that she had made the request. And in answer to your other question, she left, at the very most, five minutes ago. She was moving fast." He heard April chuckle. "But Miranda's been telling me for weeks about that deadline of hers. So I know time is of the essence."

"It sure is. Thanks, April."

He disconnected and sped up to Dex. "What's the plan?"

"We don't have the time to waste running the four blocks to base. Somebody's going to meet us near in the Grinder Parking lot."

"Who?"

"Whoever can get their ass there the fastest."

Livvie had to be picking up on her stress levels,

because she normally didn't cry like this. She was a happy baby. Of course, she wasn't in her normal car seat, either.

"Sweet Girl, we're almost home," Miranda crooned.

She hated this. She looked at Livvie in the rearview mirror. Her daughter's face was scrunched up, her tiny hands clenched into fists as she struggled against the belt on the booster seat.

"Out," her little girl sobbed.

"I'll make you smores when we get home," Miranda bribed. She had always sworn she wouldn't stoop to bribery if she'd had a child. That had flown out the window real quick.

"Out," Livvie cried again.

Miranda saw Maple street coming up. *Thank you, Lord.*

Her phone rang.

Shit, shit, shit.

She saw it over there in the footwell. She pulled over to the curb and put the car into park. Then she snagged the phone.

It wasn't the blocked number, it was Kane's number.

"Where's Griff?" she answered.

"Where are you?"

"I'm on my way home. My ETA is two minutes. I'll be safe there. Our security system is state of the art, and I'm getting the gun out of the gun safe. I'm not taking any chances with my daughter. When will Griff be home?"

"Stay on the line this time," Kane commanded.

Miranda rolled her eyes. These men. As soon as

they thought it was some kind of mission, they all sounded the same.

"I told you, now that I have Livvie and I've got my house in sight, I've got this under control. I just want my husband."

She reached up to depress the garage door opener and realized it was Susan's. Her lower lip started to tremble in frustration. She slammed the car into park and shoved on the emergency brake when she pulled into the small driveway.

"Out," Livvie shouted, when Miranda opened her door.

"In a second love, Mommy's got to open the garage door the manual style."

She ran up to the keypad by the door and pressed in the code. Then she ran back to Susan's mini-van while the garage door started to open.

"Out," Livvie shouted again.

"Dammit." Miranda managed not to raise her voice as the stuffed giraffe hit the back of her head.

"Miranda, what's wrong?" Kane demanded.

"I have a pissed off almost-two-year-old who's throwing things."

She pulled into her garage.

"Let me call you when I'm in the house and have Livvie settled. In the meantime, get my husband on the call, too." She pressed the button on the side of her phone to end the call. She got out of the driver's door and ran up to the front of the garage and depressed the garage door button. In the dim light of the garage she gave a sigh of relief. They were locked in. She opened the door to the house and turned on the hallway light and propped it open with her purse, then turned back to the car.

"Honey, we'll get you a smores, and juice, and check your diaper. Heck, I'll do anything you want, if you'll just quit crying. What can Mommy do for you?" Miranda asked as she opened the backseat door.

She leaned in and unbuckled Livvie who was sobbing.

"Ahhh, Honey. We're home now. It's going to be all right." And it was. She was home. She was safe.

She hoisted Livvie's diaper bag over one shoulder, and then gently picked up her daughter who slumped into her arms.

"Oh, you just wanted to be held, didn't you, Sweetheart?" She breathed in Livvie's scent. God, she loved her daughter. She felt her bottom. Yep, she definitely needed a new diaper, Miranda grinned. It was nice that things were normal.

She hipped checked the car door to close it.

"Smore?"

"You betchya. I'm going to have one too. Mommy's due."

"Can I have one, too? I like smores."

Miranda whirled around, hugging Livvie for dear life.

"How'd you get in here?" She demanded of her father.

"I love garage doors. They go up, and you come in while the car drives in. So simple. Can I hold my granddaughter?"

"WHAT DO you mean she hasn't called you and now you can't get ahold of her?" Griff shouted at Kane.

Griff was shoved into the front seat of Dalton's beat-up, rusted, baby blue, 1990 Chevy truck, along with Dex. Dalton was going the speed limit in the little town of Coronado, because sure as shit, they'd get pulled over. They'd be able to make up time on the freeway.

"I'm saying that she's not picking up."

"Dex, do your fucking magic. I have my security system app coded into my phone. The outside surveillance is always on, so is the baby's room. If Miranda activated, the rest of the house is monitored, too."

Dex looked at him for a moment. Griff saw the exact moment where it clicked with his friend.

"Shit, Griff, I could definitely tap into that and get it downloaded to my phone if I were at my computer. I could do it fast. But I can't do it fast from my phone."

"Kane, you're a hotshot. What about you?" Griff barked.

"I'm out of the country in a shit-hole. My security sucks."

"Call Clint," Dalton said, referring to Clint Archer of Midnight Delta. He was the third communications guru of the SEAL teams. "They're not deployed." Dalton handed Griff his cell phone.

Griff went through Dalton's contacts and dialed Clint.

"What do you need, Dalton?" Clint answered.

"This is Griff Porter, I have an emergency."

"Spill it."

Griff put the phone on speaker and he explained what was going on.

"Your biggest problem is going to be overriding the system so that we can see what the hell is going on in all rooms, whether Miranda turns on that capability or not," Clint said.

"You can't," Griff said. "It's foolproof."

Dex and Clint laughed.

"Give me your passcode," Clint said. "Dex, is all the info I have on your phone still the same?"

"Fuck no, I change that shit daily."

"Sorry, stupid question. I'll pull it off of our encrypted site."

"How long is this going to take?" Griff asked.

"I'll have this app up on Clint's phone in seven minutes. We'll have visuals in every room you have a camera."

Griff would get upset about the invasion of privacy and the fact that he was sold a shitty system, some other time. Right now, he'd promise to wash Clint's truck in a bikini if he could pull this off. He looked up and realized they were about to cross the Coronado bridge. After they crossed, it would be twenty to forty-five minutes to get home, depending on traffic and speed.

Please, God.

Please, God.

As soon as they hit The Five, Dalton put on the gas,

and they were going forty over the speed limit, where everyone else was going twenty over.

His hand hit the dash as Dalton veered around a cement mixer. The seatbelt cut in hard on his ribs. The pain only made his focus clearer.

"Dalton, I need to stay alive to save my wife and kid, you got it?" he yelled.

Dalton's only response was to go faster.

HE HAD A GUN. It was Glock thirty-six, must be department issued. It was pointed down, not at her baby.

"Let's go inside."

"I'm not going anywhere when you have a gun near my child." She slumped against her car. It was negotiation one-oh-one. She needed to start exerting power from the get go.

"Move now. I'm not kidding."

"What aren't you kidding about, Heinrich? Isn't it about time you told me what you want? You certainly aren't here at my house with a gun because you want some father/daughter bonding time. Now spill it." She pretended he was an employee that she was getting ready to fire.

"I heard you were a ball-buster. Not at all like your mother. However, you're stupid. Apparently you didn't inherit my brains."

"I just want to hear you spell it out. I'm not going to assume a damn thing where you're concerned."

"Smores," Livvie kicked out.

"In just a moment, Baby." Miranda cradled her little girl's head. "You'll get smores in just a minute."

"No she won't, because you're going to be busy uploading all of the files for Pegasus to my virtual private server."

Miranda snorted. She'd thought as much. "You're delusional."

"No, I'm not. Many children take care of their parents in their old age. You're just taking care of me when I'm in my prime, and I appreciate it. I really do." His smile made her skin crawl.

"Not going to happen. Hell, even if I wanted to. Even if you put that gun to my head and threatened to blow my brains out, I couldn't do it. I don't have access to the files at the house, and the encrypted files are of the type that they can't be copied. My God, how stupid *are* you?"

He lifted the gun and took five swift steps toward her, aiming at Livvie, Miranda twirled around and hunched over, sheltering her baby against the safety of her SUV and her body. He wormed the gun between them, pressing it against Livvie's squirming body as the little girl screamed.

"Just try me. I'll kill her. You don't give me what I want, I'll kill your brat."

The word 'brat' echoed in her brain.

"You mean like you wanted my mother to kill me?" she hissed.

He smiled slowly. "Guess that would have been a

mistake, what with you being in a position to help me. But your *brat* is of no use to me, and don't you forget it."

"Yes she is. She's your leverage." A fear like she'd never known racing through her body. She had to be smart. She had to be brave. It was the only thing that would keep her daughter alive. That and Griff.

"Then bitch, you better think of something to give me what I want. Because, me being in a situation where I have nothing to lose, means I'll kill her for sport. You better do something to give me some hope."

She desperately wanted to put some of the self-defense moves that Griff had hammered home into play. He was so close she knew he'd had garlic at lunch and hadn't flossed for days. Couldn't she turn around and kick his nuts into his lungs?

Thousands of years of maternal instincts overrode everything else and she spoke.

"I need to think, Roger, You need to let me think." Her voice was quiet.

"Dad. Call me Dad."

"Dad," she choked out a whisper.

"Good girl," he slowly withdrew the gun from Livvie's side. The little girl's sobs were heartbreaking. Heinrich walked carefully backwards, his gun trained on the two of them. "You go on ahead. I'll follow," he said in a jovial voice.

14

SHE SLOW-WALKED INTO THE HOUSE.

"Speed it up."

"I can't. I'm in heels. Livvie's squirming too much."

She went down the short hall to the living room and dropped her purse and the diaper bag then made a turn to the left.

"Uh-uh, I see a desk over there in the corner."

"I have to change her, otherwise we're never going to get a moment of peace."

Heinrich kicked at the diaper bag. "So change her."

"I'm going to her bedroom and getting her changed, washed and into a change of clothes. She's soaked through. Deal with it. You want me to think of something, then I need a moment to actually *to do just that!*"

She needed ten moments to think, and she needed to stall for time. Griffin would come through, she knew he would. Somehow, some way, her husband would be here.

Stall, Miranda, Stall.

"Fine, let's go to the kid's room."

Miranda went down the hall with Livvie crying and snuffling into her neck. She was so tired that she couldn't even keep up a good tantrum.

"It's okay, Love. It's all going to be okay," she whispered softly so only her daughter could hear. She stroked the silky strands of black hair on her hot head. Maybe she could get Livvie into her crib and close the door and wrestle the gun away from Heinrich. Anything to stop the asshole from harming her child. What did it matter if she died, as long as Livvie were alive?

What was she thinking? She was damn well going to live and raise her daughter!

"Smore?" Livvie said drowsily against her neck.

"In a minute, Love. In a minute." She forced her voice to be upbeat. "First we're going to get you cleaned up and sweet smelling, how does that sound? What would you like to wear? Pink?"

"Pik?" She rolled her head and pushed up so she could look up at her mom. She gave a wobbly smile. "Pik, Mama."

It was a new word for Livvie. She loved pink.

"Hurry up. I don't have time for this shit."

Livvie whimpered.

Miranda responded in a singsong voice. "If you stop being an asshole, I might be able to clean, feed and get my daughter to sleep. Then I can see about getting my assistant to send the files to my home e-mail. So how about it Daddy, think you can keep your shit together?"

All the time she nuzzled Livvie as she stepped through the nursery door to the far wall where the changing table was. But it wasn't working, Livvie started to squirm and squeak her displeasure, once again sensing Miranda's mood.

Miranda almost dropped Livvie onto the table when the gun was jabbed into her back.

That *was going to leave a bruise.*

"Bitch, you know your mother had a smart mouth too. I didn't like it. So shut up. Shut your kid up, and get me what I need. I don't like kids, and I'm not above hurting *yours* to keep you in line."

At Heinrich's staccato delivery, Livvie stopped making any sounds, it was like her little girl knew that there was trouble and she needed to keep quiet. She was her father's daughter.

"Okay. I just need three minutes, then I'll get to the office desk," she said quietly.

"WE'RE IN." Dex thrust his phone at Griff. The app worked the same way.

"So did Miranda turn on camera's for the entire house?" he asked as he looked at his living room.

"No," Dex and Clint said simultaneously. Clint spoke through Dalton's phone.

Griff started flipping through the pictures on the app, and when he got to Livvie's room, spiders crawled down his spine. The camera was set at an angle where you could see his baby girl's crib. He could see

Miranda's back where she was bending over Livvie at the changing table, and behind her was Roger Heinrich. Because of the position, he couldn't see what was between them, but his body language indicated he was holding a weapon.

Dex was pressed up against Griff. "Blow up the image," Dex said.

Griff shook his head, clearing it. He enlarged the picture on the phone. He still couldn't see the weapon that was trained on Miranda, but he could see that she was unharmed, her shoulders were tight under the light sweater she'd worn to work. He could see her pulling on leggings for Livvie.

Griff looked up to see where they were on the freeway, he saw the slow down ahead. Too damn far away. "Who's close to Poway?"

"I've been checking," Clint called over Dalton's phone. "I've already got the cavalry going over to your place. "Commander McAllister and Captain Hale were in a meeting at Miramar, I pinged them. The Captain is going to be calling Dex's phone."

"Well stop him," Griff yelled. "I don't want to interrupt this feed. Why the hell isn't he patching through you?"

Griff did a quick calculation in his head. Miramar was definitely closer to his house in Poway, than the base in Coronado, and looking at the traffic ahead of them on The Fifteen freeway, they were going to be another hour."

"Dalton, in about five miles is the Pamerado exit. Take that."

Dalton blasted his horn, and started squeezing over. People took one look at his truck and figured he wouldn't care if he banged into them, so they got the hell out of his way. Soon he was driving on the shoulder, once again going way, way faster than anybody else was going. Dalton took the Pamerado exit on two wheels, and Griff suppressed a groan as the seat belt cut into his rib.

"What now?" Dalton asked.

"The main intersections are Sprint, Scripps then take a right on Poway. Dex, take the call from Josiah, I don't have time for that shit until he gets to the house." He lowered his head and sucked in a breath as he saw his beautiful wife pick up their precious baby.

A grin spread over his face as he saw her head to the crib. Livvie was having a fit, she sure as hell didn't want to be put down for a nap, but Miranda didn't care. She set their crying daughter on her plump butt and gave her a pacifier.

Go Miranda!

He saw Heinrich get in Miranda's face, it was clear he didn't want Miranda to leave Livvie in the nursery. He watched his woman throw her hands on her hips and go nose to nose with the guy. Good for her. God he loved his wife. Finally Heinrich gave in, and he followed her out the nursery door. Griff's heart sank when he got a good look at the Glock he was holding on Miranda. It made it all real.

Griff switched to the hallway cam, and watched as they went to the living room. There were two in there, one that showed the main seating area, and one near the corner with the desk. Why was he not surprised that's where they ended up? This *had* to be about the project she'd been working on. He didn't know what it was, but it was *big*.

He watched as she sat down at the desk. She looked up at him. Then he saw it. That damned mutinous expression.

No Baby, cooperate. Please, come on. It's not worth it.

Heinrich was getting all worked up. He saw it. The picture was in black and white, but Griff imagined he could see him getting red in the face as he started to yell. Miranda tried to get up from the chair. He shoved her down.

She shouted back at him.

Time came to a slow crawl as Griff saw him take his pistol and slash it across her cheek. Her head whipped backwards, and she fell out of the chair. He could swear he had heard a crack. Had the monster actually broken her cheek?

When Heinrich bent down, Griff saw him use his left hand to tangle it in Miranda's hair to wrench her up. She grabbed his hand and pulled him down, her feet in his stomach and he waited with baited breath.

Come on. You can do it. You can do it.

But Heinrich countered the move. He didn't let her push him over her head. Instead he broke her hold, stood up, and kicked her in the ribs. Then he grabbed her arm and shoved her back into the chair. She sat there sullen. He made a move to the hallway, in the direction of Livvie's room. Griff saw Miranda struggle to stand. She was screaming. Heinrich turned, a look of satisfaction on his face. He meandered back to her, his gun pointed at her. She bowed her head and sat back down.

Griff looked up to orient himself. Two more stoplights and they would be taking a right onto Poway, then ten minutes to home.

THINGS WERE soft around the edges.

She just knew she was going to need some of her crowns re-done, the fucker. Miranda chose to focus on anger and hate. She would not give into pain and fear.

She would not.

After all, she'd managed to talk him away from Livvie...again.

Where was Griff?

Stop it. He's going to be here.

"Hand me my purse," she pointed to the black bag that she'd dropped near the hallway. I have my VPN tag on my keychain.

He gave her a questioning stare.

"It is my little fob that has numbers that are constantly changing, so I can access our virtual private network securely. Every employee has one, mine allows me a higher clearance than most. But I can't download anything to this hard drive, nor can I make copies or screenshots."

She damn near rolled her eyes at his look of desolation. Seriously, it didn't occur to him to take pictures with his I-Phone of her computer screen? She couldn't possibly be related to this numbnut.

He grabbed her purse and rifled through it. When he found the keys, he thrust them at her.

"Get the files up. I want to see them. I want to make sure you're not jacking me around."

"Who's your client, Dad?"

"None of your damn business."

"This is big stuff. Are you getting your money's worth?" Her words were coming out slurred. She wouldn't be able to talk much longer. She looked down at the numbers on the VPN, they weren't clear.

Please God, say she wasn't about to lose consciousness, she needed to stay awake to ensure her Hope's safety.

Keep it together, Miranda. You're in your home, and this is about Livvie. Not Hope. You're not on the train.

"I'm getting more than money, I'm getting my life back. Now hurry up, I want to see those plans."

She connected to her secure home internet, and then used the company VPN fob. She saw her desktop. She was in!

"Show me." He had his phone out. Was he going to take pictures?

She opened up the overall Pegasus file, but moved to the one from four weeks ago, the one with the flaws. She opened up that schematic. She got up real close to her screen so that she could see the screen clearly. Her right eye was almost swollen shut.

Heinrich was on the phone. "Mr. Cheong,"

Heinrich said deferentially. "I have the Pegasus schematics. I've done as you've requested, Sir."

Miranda watched Heinrich's entire demeanor change before her eyes, the bully was gone, in his place was a man who had obviously been bullied. He was the lowest person on the totem pole.

"Yes Sir."

He nodded again.

"Yes Sir."

He pulled a pen out of her cup, then grabbed an envelope off her desk and started writing notes.

"Uhmm." Heinrich was silent.

Finally he continued. "She says that can't be done."

Slowly he lowered the phone and pressed the button so that it was on speaker. "He wants to talk to you."

"I know you, Miranda Porter, you have an important role with Pegasus, you don't work with the Lartronics, but you'll do."

"Who are you?" Miranda demanded. She squinted to see if she could recognize the number. She couldn't see. It too was blocked. What she did notice is that it had only been fifteen minutes since she'd looked at the car dash clock. Dammit, Griff was still probably another twenty minutes away, and he had no idea how bad it had gotten.

"What do you mean, I'll do?" Her words came out garbled.

"You're the Project Manager at TAID, you have Top Secret Clearance. My government is interested in what you can provide. Mr. Heinrich has been promising to deliver us these plans for quite some time. It wasn't until we started taking more drastic measures that he knew we getting impatient."

He saw Heinrich pale. "Burning down my house wasn't necessary," he whined.

There was the whiner she had first known.

"Nonsense, we're finally close to getting the deliverable. Now Mrs. Porter, please upload these files to the location that Heinrich has written down."

She let out a broken laugh to go with her broken face. "Look, I told Henrich." She sneered at the toad. "Our system has too many fail-safes. It doesn't allow you to download to any computers other than four secure comps at TAID headquarters, and it sure as hell doesn't allow you to make copies." The last word sounded like she said coffees. She pulled out some tissues from the box on her desk and pressed them against her mouth.

"Then it's you I need." Cheong said easily.

"What?"

What was he talking about.

Her doorbell rang.

"Answer the door Mr. Heinrich."

Her father looked like he was going to throw up.

"If you don't do this, it will only get worse."

Heinrich hung up the phone.

"Is there a back way out of here?" he demanded hoarsely.

Miranda stumbled up out of her chair and ran to Livvie's room. She burst through the door, and God love her, Livvie remained asleep. She frantically looked around.

"Hurry up," as the doorbell sounded again.

She picked up Livvie who was dead weight. Perfect, it was better than her squirming. She also snatched her baby blanket. She veered to the master bedroom, and yanked open the top drawer of the dresser. She found Griff's light weight body armor.

She placed Livvie on the bed.

"Mama?" Her baby girl hated it when she tried to encase whole body in the too big black vest.

"No."

"It's Daddy's." Miranda smiled, then wrapped the blanket around her squirming girl. This so wasn't going to work, but it was the only thing she could think of.

"Bitch, let's go." Heinrich was at the bedroom door waving his gun.

The room was spinning, but Miranda could do anything for her daughter.

The sound of Heinrich's voice startled Livvie from the start of a tantrum. Once again, her daughter caught on that there was a problem.

15

"We're on Poway, now what?" Dalton demanded.

"Four lights, then a left," Dex answered absently. He was looking over Griff's shoulder at the drama playing out on the small phone screen.

"Beautiful," Griff breathed out through gritted teeth. He only wished he'd had two vests at home. How had Miranda gotten Livvie to put up with that shit? His wife was brilliant.

"Griff, why are they headed to your patio door?" Dex asked. "Check your porch."

He did. He didn't like what he was seeing. Three big Eurasian men were standing on the porch. One started to pound on the door with his fist, he was yelling something. It was the first time Griff regretted being able to afford a property that was further back from the street with space between his neighbors.

The one pounding at the door, pointed at the other two, and they took off going on either side of the house.

"It's not far to your neighbor's backyard if they go

out your backdoor," Dex said as Heinrich followed Miranda to the sliding glass door. She pointed to the computer and asked a question. Heinrich grabbed her and then pushed her toward the door.

Dalton blew through a red light, oblivious to the horns honking. Dalton's phone rang.

"Is that your piece of shit truck that just ran the red light?" Josiah Hale wanted to know.

Dalton glanced in his rear view mirror.

"Is that your NSX behind me?"

"No, it's Liam's. He wants to know what you have under your hood."

"Quit with the chit chat, we're three minutes from the house," Griff ground out loudly. "We have one bad guy with a gun trained on my wife and baby inside the house. Three bogeys outside, one at the front door, two went to scout the perimeter on either side. Bad guy and Miranda are heading out the back door."

"What else?" Josiah demanded.

They were coming up on Maple.

"Dalton, we need to slow down, your truck's too loud."

"I'm way ahead of you," Dalton said to Griff, as he downshifted and took the vehicle down to a purr. "Where should I park?"

"Dalton, we're going to go one more street down and actually take a right onto Evergreen. I want to get to the back of the yard."

"Gotchya."

"Josiah have Liam park two houses before my home, on Maple," Griff said.

"Affirmative." Josiah answered.

Griff watched as Miranda and Livvie and the piece-of-shit Heinrich stepped out of the patio door. Heinrich was hit from behind, not on the head, no the big man went for a kidney a hard kidney punch for maximum pain, and Heinrich went down like a sack of potatoes. Griff grinned ferally.

He then grabbed Miranda by the hair and yanked downwards so she went to her knees. Griff felt like he was falling off a cliff when he saw the man pull out a sub-machine gun from his jacket. He jammed it into her side, right next to Livvie. He whispered into Miranda's ear. She nodded, and nodded again, clutching a crying Livvie to her bosom. He saw the tears streaming down his wife's face.

He needed to get to her. Another man came up beside her. He had a gun trained on her too. Griff swept right twice on the app and saw that the first guy was still on the porch, now he had a phone to his ear. But then he took a leap off the porch, and went to hide behind the big agave and other succulent plants that grew to the right of the of the house's exterior. Fat lot of good it did, since there was a huge Escalade in the front driveway, it was a bit of a giveaway.

"Josiah, bogey to the right of the porch. Just pulled a sub-machine gun. Bizon. Fucker looks like he's one of the Gurkha mercs we've been hearing about. Watch yourself."

"On it," Liam said.

"What in the hell is Miranda working on?" Josiah asked.

"Top Secret, with DOD. I know she's giving her findings to a general who's presenting to the Joint Chiefs of Staff."

Liam whistled.

"So this could be the Chinese or Russians who want this," Josiah muttered.

"Yep," Dex answered.

Dalton pulled to a stop where Griff pointed. They had pulled up at the Norton residence. Peggy Norton was a widow, and she always knew what was going on, but he hadn't heard Peaches, her dog for the last three days, so maybe she was out of town.

Please, say they'd caught a break.

"What's the plan?" Dalton asked.

"We're going through the side fence," Griff said as he hopped out of Dalton's truck. He ignored the stab of pain in his ribs. "Follow me." He hot-footed it to the gate and reached over for the latch. Nope, no barking. This was good.

He looked behind him. Why the hell was Dalton crouched in the back of his pick-up truck at his toolbox? They didn't have time to spare, didn't he realize that?

Fuck him.

Dex followed Griff through the yard. They peeked over the fence, their guns drawn. It was hell on the other side. Miranda was wrestling with one of the men as he tried to pull Livvie from his arms.

"You want my help, then don't take my daughter," she yelled.

He had her head tipped back, gripping her hair. He was damn near spitting in her bloody, swollen face.

"Maybe I just cut baby, make you work faster? Huh?" He laughed. "Cheong wants the files, and if you don't give to him, I kill baby."

"You kill her, and you can kill me too. I won't care what you do to me, it won't matter anymore."

Heinrich was lying on the grass. He grabbed the second man's leg. "I can help. Tell Cheong I'm useful. I know how to get into her files."

The man holding Miranda looked down for just a moment. Griff hesitated, he wanted to take the shot so badly, but he couldn't risk it. He needed to separate Miranda from the mercenaries. How?

Dalton came up behind him. Griff spared him a quick glance, then did a double take.

"What the hell?"

"After the Tahoe incident, I'm not leaving home without some firepower." Dalton handed Dex an M14, but Griff praised God when Dalton handed him the MK12 sniper rifle.

"I'll take the one fighting with the guy, you take the one with Miranda," Dex said.

"Get Josiah on the phone." Griff commanded. The last thing he needed was yelling or shooting from the front of the house.

Dex explained the situation to their captain.

"Okay, they're standing down, but keeping that guy in their sites. Do you have an idea on how to separate Miranda from the merc?" Dex asked.

Griff looked over the fence. He saw the four of

them. Five if you counted his daughter hugged so tightly to Miranda she looked to be a part of her.

Dalton darted over a few yards across the lawn and picked something up, then he came back holding a chewed up yellow tennis ball. "What do you think, will this work?"

Griff eyed it and nodded. "Throw it from over in that corner, it should get them to point their guns that way."

Please baby, drop down when they turn.

Please baby.

I'm begging you Miranda.

As soon as she saw the sub-machine gun, the ability for higher thought had left her. This close the bullets would rip through Griff's body armor and tear Livvie's fragile body apart. What was she going to do?

How long had it been now? How long?

Griff!

She yanked back her head so she could look down at Livvie, she needed to see her daughter. "Let me go," she cried.

"You will help me?" He breathed in her face.

"Yes."

He let go of her hair.

She looked down, she was holding Livvie too tight. She saw that she was sweating and panting. She pushed back her blanket just enough so that she wasn't covering her face, but not far enough to expose the vest.

"Livvie?"

Her head lolled.

"She needs water," Miranda wept.

"Computer," the man leaning over her demanded.

"I can help," Heinrich whimpered.

Maybe he could. She saw that the other thug was enjoying kicking him. "Stop, I need him. He has to tell me where to upload the files. But first water for my baby."

"We go inside," the big man said. He grabbed her hair again, but it was too much. She hurt. The kick she'd taken from Heinrich forced her to double over, and he lost his grip.

Miranda thought she saw a flash of yellow, and the man turned. She took the opportunity to head for the ground and she heard a loud report of a gunshot, then another, and then a never-ending echo of shots. A stream of liquid burst against the side of her face, and she shrieked, losing her balance, still trying to cover Livvie without suffocating her.

"Miranda!"

It was Griff!

The trembling didn't stop. She rolled over onto her back. She gagged when she saw the dead eyes of her father, bullets holes ripped through his entire body.

"Livvie, please help Livvie," she begged through her swollen mouth and tears as Dex's face wavered above her.

"Get water," Griff yelled to someone.

She pushed herself over on her side, the pain was excruciating.

"Easy Miranda," let me help Dex said.

She leaned against her husband's teammate as she watched Griff grappling with Livvie, tugging at the vest. Then he was gently pulling her arms out of her tiny pink T-shirt. Dalton dove to his knees beside them, picking up the shirt and pouring water on it. Griff grabbed it, and started patting her everywhere.

"Munchkin? Honey? How you doing?" Griff's voice was desperate.

She started to squirm, and he lifted her a little.

"Livvie, are you all right?" Griff asked again.

"Dada."

"Yeah, honey. I'm right here."

Then she let out an angry cry. Her little girl was working her way to a true tantrum. It was the most beautiful sound that Miranda had ever heard.

EPILOGUE

GRIFF LOOKED AROUND THE HOSPITAL WAITING ROOM, IT was déjà vu all over again. There was Beth and Jack Preston, and Jack had even brought something from the Snack Shack. Mason, Sophia and Billy. He was flanked by his parents, with his mom holding Livvie. Kenna was new as she stood by Dex, Josiah and-

"Mr. Porter?" A nurse walked into the crowded room. He jumped to his feet and rushed over.

"Yes?"

"Sorry for taking so long. We were with another patient. Your wife is doing fine. She's in recovery, come this way."

He turned to his mom. "Mom, can you bring Livvie, in about fifteen minutes, she's going to want to see her."

Claudia nodded. "Now go," she waved him on.

They'd had to do surgery to stop the bleeding in one of her kidneys. It was a damn good thing that Roger Heinrich had died that day at the hands of the

Chinese espionage ring, otherwise Griff would have been obliged to kill him. The man at the front door had been captured by Liam and Josiah and was singing a tune about a Chinese national by the name of Cheong. Apparently he was working out of Montreal to gather US military technology.

Josiah said that they had a lead on a huge network, that Cheong was just a small cog.

Just how far down the hall was Miranda?

"She's the last room on this floor," the nurse said. "One of my fellow nurses told me to expect you to spend the night, so I wanted to give you a quiet room."

"How's she doing?" Griff asked.

"She's doing a lot better than I would have thought."

That's Miranda he smiled, as he touched his ribs.

"Did you wince?" The nurse asked.

"It's nothing."

She stopped in the middle of the hall and put her hands on her hips. "Wait a minute. When one of you Navy types shows any indication of pain, it's something. What is it?"

"I might have a bruised rib," he admitted reluctantly.

"Broken rib, got it. I'll send someone in to tape it."

He glared at her. She glared back.

He liked her.

"Now can I see my wife?"

The nurse opened the door and Griff walked in. There was Miranda, in a hospital bed again.

"For the love of God," he roared. "Get off that damn phone!"

"I've got to go Evan," she said into the receiver and then winced when she tried to put it down on the bed stand holder. He snatched it away from her and slammed it down.

"What was so important that you couldn't wait until you were out of anesthesia to make a call?"

"I wanted to see how the meeting went? I already talked to your mom while you were debriefing with Josiah, and I know that Livvie checked out."

God grant him patience. Did he say Type A women turned him on?

It really was déjà vu all over again. Only this time she didn't have her laptop in the hospital room. But she'd saved a little girl, only this time it was their daughter.

He gave her a once over.

Her right eye was swollen shut, but her left eye was open, her blue eye shined at him. She smiled at him, and held out a hand. "You saved me. Again."

"You're a hero. Again." He smiled.

Tears welled in her eye.

"Hey, what's this?"

"Even after the wreck, I've never been so scared. The only thing that got me through, was knowing that you would save us."

He bent down and touched his lips to hers, wanting to give her a gentle kiss of comfort. She let go of his hand, and pulled him close, her mouth flowering open.

He needed this. He needed this connection with the woman who owned his soul. When she tried to arch even closer, he calmed her, crooning words of comfort and love.

"I think I want us to go away, and stay close together. I want you and Livvie within hands reach for at least two weeks."

"You mean I won't have to coerce you into spending time with me when you get out of the hospital, like three years ago?" he teased.

"I still don't exactly remember how you talked me into moving in with you the first time, but it was the best thing that ever happened to me. Thank you so much for loving me, even though it took me so long to get here."

He pushed a tendril of hair behind her ear. "Huh?"

"I know that it took me a long time to figure everything out. Thank you for waiting for me, and giving me the chance to grow up, and never giving up on me."

He felt like his heart would burst out of his chest. She'd always been his soulmate, and now she knew it too.

"Miranda, there was never a chance of me giving up on you. Never. You're my woman, you have been since I first saw you on that train."

Her smile bloomed like sunshine.

THANK you for reading *Her Honorable Hero*. For more Military Romance check out my Midnight Delta series. *Her Vigilant SEAL*, Book 1 is free.

Get your copy of Her Vigilant SEAL here.

ABOUT THE AUTHOR

USA Today Bestselling Author, Caitlyn O'Leary, adores writing Military Romantic Suspense and Paranormal Romance. She started publishing books in 2014. Storytelling has been a tradition in her family for years, and she still holds on to the letters she has received from family members since her childhood.

Caitlyn lives in California with her husband John of sixteen years who often makes guest appearances in her reader group, Caitlyn's Crew. Getting to know so many people within the reader community is almost as much fun as writing each new novel. So join her reader group so she can get to know you, and see if she and John can make it to year seventeen!

You never know what kind of book she'll write next, it all depends on what strikes her fancy. Be sure to keep in touch.

Keep up with Caitlyn O'Leary:

Website: www.caitlynoleary.com
Email: caitlyn@caitlynoleary.com
Newsletter: http://eepurl.com/c5FqPv

facebook.com/Caitlyn-OLeary-Author-
638771522866740

twitter.com/CaitlynOLearyNA

instagram.com/caitlynoleary_author

amazon.com/author/caitlynoleary

bookbub.com/authors/caitlyn-o-leary

goodreads.com/CaitlynOLeary

pinterest.com/caitlynoleary35

ALSO BY CAITLYN O'LEARY

THE MIDNIGHT DELTA SERIES

Her Vigilant Seal (Book #1)

Her Loyal Seal (Book #2)

Her Adoring Seal (Book #3)

Seal with a Kiss (Book #4)

Her Daring Seal (Book #5)

Her Fierce Seal (Book #6)

A Seals Vigilant Heart (Book #7)

Her Dominant Seal (Book #8)

Her Relentless Seal (Book #9)

Her Treasured Seal (Book #10)

BLACK DAWN SERIES

Her Steadfast Hero (Book #1)

Her Devoted Hero (Book #2)

Her Passionate Hero (Book #3)

Her Wicked Hero (Book #4)

Her Guarded Hero (Book #5)

Her Captivated Hero (Book #6)

Her Honorable Hero (Book #7)

THE FOUND SERIES

Revealed (Book #1)

Forsaken (Book #2)

Healed (Book #3)

SHADOWS ALLIANCE SERIES

Declan

FATE HARBOR SERIES

Trusting Chance (Book #1)

Protecting Olivia (Book #2)

Claiming Kara (Book #3)

Isabella's Submission (Book #4)

Cherishing Brianna (Book #5)

Printed in Great Britain
by Amazon

38756436R00131